A RAGE
OF
DEATHS

A RAGE OF DEATHS

ROBERT COBURN

A JACK HUNTER MYSTERY

ABSOLUTELY AMAZING eBOOKS

ABSOLUTELY AMAZING eBOOKS

Published by Whiz Bang LLC, 926 Truman Avenue, Key West, Florida 33040, USA.

For information contact:
Publisher@AbsolutelyAmazingEbooks.com

ISBN-13: 978-1945772764 (Absolutely Amazing Ebooks)
ISBN-10: 194577276X

To Laura.

A RAGE
OF
DEATHS

CHAPTER 1

"**WHEN DID SHE DIE?**"

"Four days ago, Jack."

"Where'd you get my number?"

"Social media."

Jack Hunter sat up from the chaise lounge by the pool. He was renting a townhouse in Porter Court, a gated compound of townhouses in Truman Annex.

He had recently been in Cuba. He and an old friend, Bobby Sunshine, had sailed there on Bobby's boat, the *Joyful Noise*. It'd been an interesting trip but now he was back in town and looking for a new home. His old landlady, Ruth LaVere, had returned to Key West and had moved back into the little house he'd lived in on Ashe Street. Before visiting Cuba, he'd spent a short stint staying on Bobby's boat at Key West Bight – until someone showed up there intending to kill him.

Now he had his eye on a small condo in Harbour Place, a few blocks down the street that was soon coming on the market. The top floor unit of a security building had a certain appeal considering the way his life had been running lately.

"I'm sorry, Leslie," Jack said, "but you know it's been years now since mom and I even spoke."

"I've always regretted that, Jack. Never could understand the animosity between you and Sarah."

Leslie was Jack's uncle. His brother had been Jack's father. The two men were identical twins and in their younger days often switched identities just for laughs. They'd once played that joke on Sarah, which eventually became a burden Jack carried throughout his childhood and even to this day.

"The funeral is in New Jersey," Leslie said. "Bloomfield cemetery near Montclair. She'll be buried next to your dad. Same people that took care of him are handling it. Maybe you'd like to come?"

Jack took in a breath as painful memories returned. He thought he'd gotten past all of that.

"Don't think so, Leslie."

"Well, I'm sorry, Jack. Love to see you. Take care of yourself."

"You, too."

Jack ended the call. Had he been too harsh just now? He looked at his phone. It'd captured the number. He could call his uncle back. Sucking in another breath, he stuck it in his left shirt pocket. A similar stainless-steel phone case carried there had once stopped a bullet and saved his life.

Two men and a woman entered the pool area pulling roller bags. They went to the condo across from him. It was also a rental so he figured they were vacationers. One man was older, perhaps the same age as Leslie. He had obviously dyed hair. The other was much younger and probably the husband of the woman. She was very attractive. He unlocked the door and held it open. Jack, to his surprise, saw the older man pat the woman's bottom as they went in.

Jack's phone chimed. He saw it was Billy Bean.

"Hey, what's up?"

Billy was Jack's business partner in two restaurants on the island.

"Fellow in here says he has a new band called Torment," Billy said. "Might be good for the Undrinkable Bar."

The Undrinkable Bar was part of the Inedible Cafe. Their other restaurant was Stella by Starlight.

"Torment? What kind of music do they play?"

"Kind you like, Jack. Jazz. Said he'd named the band Torment 'cause his teenage daughter can't stand the stuff, hee-hee."

"Book 'em, Billy," Jack laughed.

Jack lingered a little longer and was about to go inside when the younger man came out of the house.

"Hi," Jack called out and waved. "Welcome to Porter Court."

The man looked over to where Jack was sitting. He slipped on his sunglasses and saying nothing, walked out the gate. A car drove off a moment later.

Jack figured him for the rental agent. And not very friendly.

Next thing, the older man and woman stepped out. The man looked like he could use some quality time at the gym. He was wrapped in a white terrycloth bathrobe. She wore a sheer beach top that revealed a curvaceous body.

"Hello, how are you?" she called over to Jack in an exotically glossed accent. "Nice day, isn't it."

"Yes, a very nice day," Jack agreed, getting to his feet.

The man said something to her and tossed a haughty sneer at Jack. They both settled on the lounges without speaking another word. The old guy seemed to drift off.

Jack decided to give them their privacy and went inside to get dressed.

~ ~ ~

Detective Earl Gleason was writing an investigative report at the police station when his cellphone sang *I Shot the Sheriff*. The area code on the caller ID said he should let it ring through to voice mail. Against his better judgment he answered.

"Hello, Charlotte," he said.

His sister in Bradenton. A sharp divide had existed between them since his divorce. Charlotte was a close friend of the ex-wife and had sided with her.

"I need your help, Earl. Frank's been arrested."

Gleason exhaled through his nose.

"Why was he arrested?"

"Drugs. They found them at the shop. They aren't Frank's."

How many times had he heard that one before, he thought.

"Who found the drugs, Charlotte?"

"The cops, who else?"

"Was it the Bradenton department or the Feds who arrested him?"

"Bradenton. Frank's even friendly with some of them, too. He was set up, Earl. I know it!"

A small sob.

"Does Frank have a lawyer, Charlotte?"

"Yes."

"Well, call him. He'll know what to do."

"The lawyer's a woman, Earl."

"Even better."

"Can you talk to the Bradenton police? You know Frank is a good man and your being a detective and all, they might listen."

"That's not how it works, Charlotte. Let me think about this. I'll get back to you."

He hung up and read over his report once more before signing it. Family, he thought. Checking his watch, he saw that the day was about over. Might be a good evening to sit on the porch at Vinos and contemplate this mess with a glass of merlot.

CHAPTER 2

KEY WEST NEEDED BOTH FEET planted firmly on the floor before getting out of bed the next morning. It'd been one of those nights when everyone seemed to be doing the town and every bar was crammed full until closing time.

Jack, however, was up before dawn and had taken a walk on an empty Duval Street from the Gulf of Mexico to the Atlantic Ocean. Thoughts of his mother with him every step of the way.

He'd returned to Porter Court and was sitting poolside having a cup of coffee when the woman in the condo across from him burst out of the door.

"Thank God you're there," she shouted anxiously. "Come quick!"

"What's wrong?" Jack asked, jumping up.

"He's not breathing!"

Jack ran over to her.

"Upstairs," she said, fluttering her hands. "I can't wake him."

The man lay in bed, flat on his back, eyes open and mouth agape, covers pulled down to his knees. He was nude.

"What's his name?" Jack asked.

"Dewitt."

"Mr. Dewitt," Jack shouted, shaking the still body. "Mr. Dewitt, can you hear me? Wake up, sir!"

"Dewitt's his first name," the woman corrected. "Dewitt Pittway."

Jack could see no movement of the man's chest. He placed his hand on the side of the neck for a pulse. Nothing. He roughly pulled the man off the bed, dragging the sheets with him and onto the floor where he began CPR.

"Call 911," he ordered the woman.

~ ~ ~

Dewitt Pittway was pronounced DOA at Lower Keys Medical Center. In fact, he would've been cold to the touch long before the ambulance had arrived at Porter Court. On the advice of the emergency room doctor by phone to the EMT, a defibrillator hadn't been used to revive him because the emergency team had noticed a surgical incision on Mr. Pittway's chest that indicated he possibly had a pacemaker. They didn't want to risk killing him twice.

Monica Kuun, the deceased's girlfriend, had taken a taxi to the hospital. Jack had ridden with her. They now sat alone in a small consultation room.

"Why won't they let me see him?" Monica asked impatiently. "This is terrible."

"Would you like something to drink?" Jack offered. "Coffee?"

"No, I just want everything to be over."

A nurse's aide knocked on the door and entered.

"Mr. Pittway is ready," she said.

She led them to a curtained-off space in the emergency room. Dewitt Pittway was stretched out on a bed with a sheet tucked up to his chin. He looked to be asleep. Monica walked over to him and placed a hand on his forehead. Jack lingered at the entrance.

"He was such a wonderful person," she said, turning to Jack. "Kind. Generous. Everyone loved him. We were going to be married. He was so looking forward to it and now..."

"Well, I'm sure he considered himself very fortunate," Jack smiled.

"It's so cold in here," she said, clasping her arms around her shoulders. "Can we leave? I need to call the family."

Jack left her in the hospital lobby to make her calls and stepped outside himself to phone for a taxi. While out there he bummed a smoke off another man. He'd given up cigarettes again. But just this once wouldn't hurt.

"They won't release him," she said angrily when Jack returned.

"I'm sorry, release who?"

"Dewitt! They won't let the undertaker come for him."

"Did they say why?"

"Something about having to wait for the medical examiner. This is bullshit!"

Jack noticed her accent had lost some of its gloss.

"There must be a mistake," he said. "I'll go see if I can find out what's going on."

The taxi pulled up just then.

Monica shook her head.

"Forget it," she said. "Just take me home."

The cab dropped them off at the Truman Annex entrance on Southard Street. It was a short walk from there to Porter Court.

"Thank you, Jack," she said when they'd arrived at the condo. "I have to call some more people."

"Let me know if you need anything," he said, then as an afterthought, "I can help you with making those phone calls, if you'd like."

"That's very kind, Jack, but it's better that I do it myself. You understand."

"Of course. Well, I'm right across the way."

Jack hung around the house for the rest of the afternoon but saw no sign of her. Maybe it wasn't a good idea for her to be alone after her ordeal. Concerned, he went over and rang the doorbell.

"Monica?" he called out. "It's Jack Hunter."

No answer. He stuck his ear close the door and listened. Not a sound. He felt in a dilemma. Was she all right? Should he call security? He rang again. He could hear the bell. He stepped back and looked up at the building. No movement at the windows or anything. Maybe she was a sound sleeper. Could've taken a pill or something. That was more likely. She'd been through a lot today. He walked back to his place.

It was getting dark and he remembered he hadn't eaten all day. For some unknown reason, he really didn't care to go to either of his restaurants. Blue Heaven was just up from the Annex on Thomas Street. On the way out he noticed a light was on upstairs at Monica's. He wondered if he should invite her to join him. He decided to let her be.

CHAPTER 3

DETECTIVE RACHEL POWERS had been the detective-on-call for the night. Her phone rang at 2:30 a.m. A stabbing on Duval Street. She arrived at the scene twenty-five minutes later. Paramedics were already there.

Duval had been blocked off between Green and Caroline Streets. A man lay across the narrow sidewalk on the corner of Charles Street, EMTs hovering over him. Several gawkers had gathered. A man without a shirt sat cuffed in the back of a squad car. An officer was talking with a woman and another man as Powers walked up.

"What's going on?" Powers asked, showing her ID.

"Fight between the one on the ground and the person in the car," the cop said. "This lady called it in. Gentleman here restrained the assailant."

"Not too wise a thing to do," Powers said to the man. "But thank you anyway."

"I instruct martial arts. The guy was pretty drunk besides."

"Do you know either of them?" she asked.

"No, my wife and I were on our way back to where we're staying when we saw the fight start. The guy in the car pulled a knife. Looks like he hurt the other one pretty bad. Hell, I thought people came down here to have a good time."

"Some people can't handle a good time," Powers said. "The officer will take your name and address. I'd appreciate it if you could come into the police station tomorrow and fill out a statement. How long are you in town?"

"We have four more days," the man said.

9

"Would ten o'clock be good? Shouldn't take long."

She gave him her business card.

"Think he's going to be all right?" the man asked, motioning to the victim who was now being loaded into the ambulance.

"I hope so."

Powers spent another twenty minutes at the scene. The assailant had been transported and she headed back to the police station to write up the incident. An hour later what would've been an assault-with-a-deadly-weapon charge had become a homicide.

"And what time did he expire?" she asked over the phone.

"Four forty-five," the emergency room doctor said. "Perforated aorta. The medical examiner will give a complete report after the autopsy. Shame. He was a young dude."

Young or old it's always a shame when stupidity takes charge, Powers thought. She began writing a new report.

They'd found a wallet on the victim. His name was Charles Gibbs. Twenty-one years old. From New Bern, North Carolina. There were some photographs. One of him with a young girl. Another of some older folks. Probably family. She'd have to notify them.

Her back was killing her. A souvenir from Iraq. She stood up and stretched. Soon the dayshift would come on duty. She went over to the coffee maker. It was a new fancy job that used individual little plastic cups of coffee. You just pop one into the receptacle, snap the lid closed and a minute later you've brewed a steaming hot mug of Joe. She and Gleason had gone in on buying the thing. Both had considered it to be a good investment, considering the two-burner hotplate in the station.

Returning to her desk she completed the new report, now a homicide. She'd inform the man in the holding cell about the change in his arrest charges when he'd sobered up.

~ ~ ~

The resident rooster at the post office on Whitehead Street announced daybreak at precisely 5:45 a.m. every morning whether it was getting light or not. Porter Court was within earshot of the grounds.

Jack hadn't minded the early call. Chickens had long ago been granted Conch status on the island, so who was he to complain? He'd gotten up, done a little house cleaning, puttered around some more and was now enjoying a morning coffee at poolside. That had become a favorite routine.

Monica came out from the condo teary eyed.

"I don't know what to do," she sobbed. "I called to ask again when I can take Dewitt home and they said not until after the autopsy."

Jack noticed the accent was completely missing.

"Maybe they need to find out what happened to him," he said. "Seems reasonable."

"Dewitt wouldn't want an autopsy. Would you?"

The question brought a small laugh from Jack.

"Oh, you think that's funny?" Monica replied. "Being cut to pieces so people can't even look at you at your own funeral? My God!"

Now a lopsided grin involuntarily crossed Jack's face. This had been a familiar reaction in certain situations all of his life. One that usually led to further complications.

"I'm sorry, Monica. No, I don't think it's funny."

She shook her head in dismay.

"Didn't look that way to me."

He reached over and patted her arm. She drew it back.

"I understand that you're upset," he said. "But an autopsy doesn't leave the person disfigured or anything. It's like having an operation."

Monica narrowed her eyes at him.

"Oh, right, they put a band aid on you when they've finished. Really, Jack."

"I believe it's a law that they're required to find out why he died," Jack said, clearing his throat.

Monica laughed harshly.

"He had a heart attack," she snapped. "What more do they want to know? There must be a million fucking heart attacks every day!"

"Guess they still have to do it."

Monica remained quiet for a moment.

"It's odd," she said at last. "Why are you defending these people?"

The accursed grin re-crossed his face.

"Defending what people?"

"The autopsists! And why must everything be a joke with you?"

CHAPTER 4

"**BRADENTON POLICE DEPARTMENT.** Officer Davis."

"Good morning, Officer Davis. This is Detective Earl Gleason with the Key West PD. Wonder if you could help me with some information?"

Gleason had finally decided to get the rundown on his brother-in-law's arrest, even though he really didn't want to get involved. It was embarrassing. He'd been awake off and on most of the night trying to make up his mind. But at the end he felt he really had no other choice. For privacy's sake, he decided to make the call at home rather than from the station.

"Sure, detective, what do you need?"

"Your department recently arrested an individual on possession with intent. Name's Frank Anderson. I'd like to talk with whoever's handling that."

"That'd be Detective Lundy. He's not in yet."

"I'll call back. It's nothing urgent."

He next refreshed the cat's water bowl, checked the dry food and saw there was enough, and left for work.

Powers stifled a yawn just as Gleason came into the detectives' room. He reacted with one of his own.

"Weird how that happens," he said, taking his seat at the homicide table. "You yawn, I yawn, we yawn."

"Long night, sir," Powers replied. "I was duty dick. Called out on a stabbing. Duval Street."

"Get whodunit?"

"Tim Malloy. He's in a holding cell at the moment."

"How's the victim?"

"He's in the morgue."

"Ah, hell. Have we done business with this Malloy character before?"

"Couple of misdemeanors."

"What about the victim? Anything on him?"

"Kid from North Carolina is all I know so far, sir. Charles Gibbs. Haven't gotten in touch with his family yet."

"How'd it go down?"

"According to the witnesses, Gibbs and Malloy were fighting and Malloy pulled a knife. Gibbs died in the ER. I'll check with some of the local bars. See if anyone remembers them."

"Malloy know he's made the big time?"

"I haven't given him the news yet. Here's the report."

"You write good reports," Gleason nodded after he'd finished reading.

"Necessary evil, sir. I've called county to reserve him a room. You want to come with me while I inform Mr. Malloy of his new status?"

"You go ahead. I left something in my car I have to get."

Gleason went to the parking lot and called Bradenton PD.

"Detective Bill Lundy, please," he said.

"Lundy," a voice answered.

"Detective Lundy. This is Earl Gleason at Key West PD. Got a minute?"

"Oh, yeah, desk said you'd called. What can I do for you?"

"You're holding a Frank Anderson on a possession charge," Gleason said. "Wonder if you could fill me in a little on that?"

Lundy hesitated.

"Is this related to a case you all are working down there?" he asked.

Gleason grimaced. This was going to be more embarrassing than he'd imagined. He'd have to confess.

"No, it's personal. Anderson's my brother-in-law. I'm hoping for some damage control. You can appreciate my situation, I imagine."

He added a small laugh to that last bit.

"Ain't that the shits?" Lundy chuckled. "Don't worry about it, man. Every family's got a joker in the woodpile somewhere. Cops are no exception. Take mine, for example. Cousin up in Jacksonville's so screwed up he gets award points every time he spends a night in jail. Another idiot, this one's a second cousin on my mother's side, can't seem to get it right, either. Has a thing for stealing cars. It's just who they are. Hasn't a damn thing to do with you. Man, the stories I could tell you about *my* family."

Gleason decided he'd better get to the point before Lundy started telling them.

"Thank you, Detective Lundy, I'm sure they'd be interesting. But can we move on? The thing is, my sister's kind of on edge about this. I can't blame her. She says no one there will talk to her. Is that true?"

"I can't divulge anything about the investigation," Lundy said frostily. "Has nothing to do with Key West. Frankly, I'm surprised you'd even ask."

"Certainly I wouldn't want you to say something that might hurt your case but I was looking at this as more of a courtesy between departments. If there is anything you can tell me that I can pass on to her, it'd be a big help."

"Then, as a courtesy, you can tell your sister that we consider her husband dirty," Lundy said, the tone getting icier than ever.

"She believes he was set up. Anything to that?"

"Set up? Aren't they all?"

Gleason thanked the detective and ended the call. Strange how Lundy had suddenly become so stiff. Maybe his cutting him off about the family talk had put his nose out of joint.

He himself had never really cared all that much for Frank. Opinionated about everything and quick to judge. Same as Charlotte. No wonder they went for each other. Perfect match. Still, that didn't make the man a criminal.

He was interrupted by his cellphone chiming. It played two bars of *I Shot the Sheriff* before he could answer.

"Gleason."

"Good morning, detective, this is Jack Hunter."

~ ~ ~

Six hundred miles away across the Gulf of Mexico in Louisiana, Burton Sachs stood staring out the window of his law office in downtown Baton Rouge. A recent call had brought disturbing news. After a moment, he returned to his desk and Googled the Monroe County Medical Examiner's office.

~ ~ ~

"Know who answered a nine-one-one at Porter Court the other day?" Gleason asked the desk sergeant.

Gleason had initially brushed off Jack Hunter's telephone call as just another instance of him sticking his nose into other people's business. But his own cop's nose had now forced him to take a further look into the incident there.

"Lemme check, detective."

"Heart attack," Gleason said.

"Oh, yeah. Here it is. Zero nine-hundred hours. Officer Johnson arrived at the scene shortly after EMT. Elderly man found unconscious. Given CPR. No response. Taken to Lower Keys. Over and out."

"That's it? Nothing about who was present?"

"No mention on the report. Wait, here it is on the back. Monica Kuun. Supposed to be a friend of the deceased. And Jack Hunter. Says here he's a neighbor. Better ask Johnson when he comes in. He's on patrol."

Gleason thanked the sergeant and went back to the detective's room. He'd talk with Officer Johnson later. Maybe give him a few pointers about report writing while he's at it.

Powers entered the room.

"Malloy's on his way to county, sir," she said. "Not a happy camper."

"Don't do the crime if you can't do the time," Gleason singsonged. "Something like that. From an old television show."

"Probably during the time of black and white TV. You remember seeing those shows at the time, sir?"

Powers smiled.

"Re-runs, detective, re-runs."

"If you say so, sir."

"Curious call from our mutual friend, Jack Hunter," Gleason said, changing the subject. "Hunter lives in Porter Court over at the Annex. Seems his neighbor had a heart attack and died. Man's girlfriend is upset because the medical examiner wants to autopsy, Hunter says. I admit calling in the ME on a plain vanilla heart attack is a little unusual."

"Why is Mr. Hunter so interested, sir?"

"Says he's just trying to help the woman. They were renting the place across from him. Just gotten there, in fact, when it happened."

"How old was the poor man?"

"Officer Johnson was first responder. His report only said the guy was *elderly*. Johnson believes anyone over thirty has one foot in the grave. Think I'll give Hardy a call."

Dr. Blake Hardy was the medical examiner for Monroe County. Though his office was in Marathon, he was no stranger to Key West. That had been especially true during a recent string of homicides in the homeless community.

Normally, when a person has obviously succumbed to natural causes there'd be no need for an autopsy unless the death was unexpected and no medical cause can be determined. Then the medical examiner may take jurisdiction over the case.

"Dewitt Pittway you say, detective? Let me read my schedule. Right. The ER doctor requested the autopsy."

"What was it that made him want one, doctor?" Gleason asked. "Thought this was just a heart attack. Elderly victim."

"Yes, that is correct. But *why* it happened is what we need to know. Calvin Wright was the ER doctor when they brought in Mr. Pittway. He pronounced the man DOA and signed the death certificate as a heart attack with a clause pertaining to underlying cause."

"So he had a heart attack and passed away before they could do anything. Doesn't make it a crime."

"That's also true. Furthermore, Dr. Wright believes the man was already dead before the EMT got there. Possibly for several hours according to the body's core temperature. Here's an interesting bit of medical trivia for you, detective. Did you know most strokes occur in the hours just before we begin to awaken? Has to do with our circadian rhythm. It's like a bear hibernating. Brain tells the body to start getting ready for the day. Heart rate increases. Blood pressure jumps. Could break loose a piece of plaque in an artery and send it where it isn't welcomed. Pittway was apparently at risk. He had a pacemaker, which should've kept him going. So either the pacemaker failed, which would mean there's a problem the manufacturer ought to know about, or possibly it hadn't been reset lately, which means Mr. Dewitt had been remiss in keeping appointments with his cardiologist. On the darker side, however, his attack could've been triggered by other means."

Gleason's interest perked at this.

"Want to throw a little light on that darker side, doc?"

"Suffocation, poison, bad nightmare, things that go bump in the night," he joked. "Here's another one. There's been some talk about hacking a pacemaker. Possible, I suppose, but that'd take an expert. Might have to go to Russia to find one."

Gleason laughed.

"Without the man's medical history, say he had a disease he was being treated for or some other condition," Hardy continued, "I'm good with plain old heart failure but we won't know for certain until we open him up. Then we can examine the heart itself and look at the pacemaker. Determine if it was up to snuff."

"When can you perform the autopsy?" Gleason asked.

"I'd thought day after tomorrow but now it looks like it'll go into next week. I've got some business in Key Largo that has first dibs."

"I wouldn't mind being there when you get around to it."

"Always a pleasure to have you, detective. I'll let you know."

CHAPTER 5

JACK GOT NOTHING from Gleason about the autopsy. That put Monica further into a snit. She laid it on him. Here she was stuck in this hellish place on the whim of some perverted doctor. She had a duty to Dewitt, were they all so blind they couldn't see that?

Jack excused himself and returned to his condo. But her mention of duty had struck a nerve with him. He booked a flight to Newark.

~ ~ ~

New Jersey had cloaked itself in winter bleakness. A late spring storm had dusted the ground with just enough snow to kill the flowering crocuses and other early bloomers. It'd also plummeted the temperature twenty degrees below normal, not counting the wind-chill factor.

Jack was ill-prepared for the weather change, having worn the only suit he still owned, a light-weight worsted wool. A carry-over from his ad agency days when he'd lived in sunny Los Angeles and was a clotheshorse.

"Came in last night," the driver said, hustling along the sidewalk to his limo. "You can always expect a little snow 'bout now. Nothin' to do with climate change. No matter what the tree huggers believe. Just the way the world turns. Car's right up ahead."

Jack pulled his jacket tighter around him as they walked from the airport terminal, the wind cruelly whipping at his legs.

"You know how to get to the cemetery?" he asked. "Bloomfield. Up near Montclair."

"Got a GPS. No problem."

"Good. The funeral's at eleven. Just stand by until it's over and then bring me back to the airport. My flight's at three."

"Gotcha covered."

Jack settled in the back seat of the limo and the warmth from the heater quickly had him nodding. They'd no sooner gotten on the Garden State Parkway when traffic came to a halt.

"Snow makes everybody nuts," the driver shrugged. "People can't drive like they used to."

Actually, the tie-up was due to a jackknifed tractor-trailer across both lanes two miles ahead. Thirty minutes passed before they'd inched to the next exit.

"We'll take surface streets the rest of the way," the driver told Jack. "Put it on autopilot and let the GPS do the driving, ha, ha."

Jack, snug in the back seat, drifted in and out of sleep. They'd passed Parsippany before he felt something was wrong.

"Pull over and check that GPS," he said. "This isn't the right way."

The driver reluctantly eased to the side of the road and stopped.

"Let me see that thing," Jack said.

"Brand new unit," the driver said smugly, removing the device from the dashboard mount. "Works like a charm."

"You put in Bloomingdale, man! I said *Bloomfield*. We're miles from there. Turn around."

Sadly, only one person was left standing at the gravesite when they finally arrived at the cemetery, the service having ended nearly an hour ago.

Jack recognized the lone elderly man.

"Hello, Lesley."

Leslie looked up, startled.

"Jack, I didn't expect you..."

"Yeah, looks like I missed the party."

The two men took in each other, separated by generations and meeting in a field of tombstones. A snow flurry swirled momentarily.

"I'm glad you came, Jack. Sarah would've been pleased."

The thought of pleasing anyone lying in a casket at a funeral caused Jack to shake his head in wonder. He walked over to the fresh grave. A couple of flower sprays stood watch.

"Well, it's finished," he said.

"Is it, Jack?"

Jack turned to his uncle.

"Your mother loved you," Leslie continued. "You may not believe it but not a day passed that she didn't think of you or mention some little memory from long ago."

"That *is* hard to believe," Jack said. "She tossed me aside the moment Howard died."

"I remember it as being the other way around, Jack. You cut her off. There was no reason to have done that."

Jack snorted a contemptuous laugh.

"Have you any idea of what it was like growing up because of the two of you?" he asked angrily. "Hey, don't try to pretend it wasn't true. I read the damn love letters you'd written each other. Bet you didn't know, huh? What've you got to say about that?"

Leslie didn't answer.

"You and Sarah were lovers all along," he grimaced. "Howard was just in the way. Same as me."

Leslie nodded.

"Okay, guess it *is* time to talk about that," he said. "I'll start with the letters. Sarah suspected it was you who'd taken them. Yes, we wrote them to each other.

Your mother and I were in love. We'd always been so from the first time we met."

"So why didn't you marry her instead of Howard? Make her an honest woman while you were at it, too."

Leslie gave Jack a painful look.

"Jack, if you were someone else, I'd punch you in the nose for saying that. An honest woman, indeed! You don't know the half of it."

"What the hell else am I supposed to believe?"

"Just shut up and listen. No woman was more straight-laced than your mother. Nor more principled. Her word was gold. Once she gave it there was no taking it back."

"Are you telling me that the old joke about you and Howard changing places the night he proposed to her and she thought it was you, yet she ... oh, give me a break!"

"That's exactly what happened, Jack. Howard fancied her. And he took advantage. But there was even more to it and that's what I'm going to tell you now. Why to this day I can never forgive him."

Jack clasped his arms around himself, the cold cutting into his ribs.

"They decided to elope that very night," Leslie continued. "Went to some dumb town out of state. Howard's idea, no doubt."

"Didn't you wonder where she was? How long were they away? Why didn't you call her?"

"They were gone for a couple of weeks. Remember, we didn't have cellphones back then. I couldn't reach Howard, either. I was out of my mind with worry. When they returned, she discovered she was pregnant with you. She couldn't bring herself to divorce Howard."

"Why the hell not? He'd deceived her."

"She believed the father should also raise the child. And she'd given her word."

"Her damn word was so precious that'd she would consent to that?" Jack asked incredulously. "Give up her true love and marry the facsimile brother? Oh, excuse me. By mistake, I should add. And me also by mistake."

"A principle isn't worth anything until it costs you. Sarah had her principles. The other thing is there was never any hanky-panky between us. She was one of those women who believed you should be married first. Another principle of hers."

"Tough having a saint for a mom," Jack sighed, "I can tell you that much. Can't imagine having one for a wife."

"She wasn't a saint, Jack. She just had strict beliefs and stuck to them."

"Regardless of how much those fucking beliefs might hurt another?" Jack asked bewilderedly. "I'd call that self-righteousness. This is difficult for me, Leslie. Sure you understand."

Leslie gestured toward his brother's headstone.

"Funny story about Howard's death," he said.

"Dropped dead at the Port Authority is what I heard," Jack said. "Sorry place to die in, if that's the joke."

"Howard liked to bowl," Leslie said. "The Port Authority had a bowling alley. He'd always dreamed of bowling a perfect game. All strikes every frame. Three hundred score. Came close a couple of times but no cigar. So Howard's at the bowling alley in the Port Authority and he's on a streak. Nine strikes in a row. Needs three more for that perfect game. First ball is a strike! Second ball another strike! Lines up for the third. Starts his approach, releases the ball – bam! Heart attack! Howard falls and skids across the foul line. Strike three! But because he'd fouled, it didn't count. Ironically, the next week some son-of-a-bitch bowled a perfect game on the very same lane."

Jack couldn't help but laugh.

"That's some story, Leslie."

"Well, like I've always said, a little humor takes the edge off anything."

"What are your plans now?"

"Think I'll stay in Baltimore for the time being."

Jack stooped and picked a flower from his mother's grave. He put it in his coat pocket.

"You need a ride anywhere?" he asked.

"My car's here but thanks."

"Well, you have my phone number. Call anytime."

"You, too, Jack. Take care."

Jack walked to his waiting limo.

"Know the way back to the airport, sport?" he asked the driver.

CHAPTER 6

GLEASON STOOD IN HIS TINY KITCHEN about to put a slice of pizza in the microwave when the phone interrupted. A tearful Charlotte on the other end with more distressing news.

The lawyer they'd originally hired for Frank had taken herself off the case, she reported. Something about a conflict of interest or other. Sounded to her like she just wanted to get out. Probably to take a better-paying case.

A moment to blow her nose.

Anyway the woman had suggested another lawyer, a man. Gave him high marks, too. Said their legal situation was right up his alley.

Well, that must be some alley was all she could say. His idea of what they should do was to make a deal. Guilty plea for a reduced sentence. In other words, sell out to the system and go to jail. Great lawyer they'd been given, huh?

The tears had turned to anger at this point.

Of course, that would be providing the City Attorney went along, the lawyer had further explained. There'd been a lot of drug crimes lately and the administration needed to make some political hay. Coming down hard on a dealer, big or small, could go a long way with the voters.

Naturally, she'd had gone ballistic over the idea of her Frank pleading guilty to something he hadn't done. The cops had set him up. It was as plain as day. Anyone with eyes could see that.

The new lawyer hadn't been impressed by her insight, however. Better to avoid a drawn-out trial with an iffy conclusion, he'd cautioned, not to mention the expense.

Gleason figured she'd finally gotten around to what was really upsetting—the expense.

He'd offered her the only advice he could – don't worry and do nothing at the moment. That'd only opened the locks for another flood of tears followed by an abrupt hang-up.

Now the cat was demanding supper and hopped from the sofa to floor.

"What a mess," he muttered.

Mitts meowed and rubbed against his leg.

The lawyer was probably right, he thought. Frank had always seemed to have had a preference for the shady side of life. Just look at what he did for a living. Ran a motorcycle shop. Bikers hanging around. Place was drugs central for all he knew.

And that was just it. He knew nothing. His dislike of the man was showing. He was better than this. At least he believed he was.

He filled the cat's dish with something vile-smelling from a can and placed it on the floor. Mitts was on it with a purr practically before he could remove his hand.

Giving a long sigh, he took the pizza out of the microwave and put it back in the refrigerator, having lost his appetite during the phone call.

"Think there's a nature program on television," he said to the cat, flicking on the TV and turning up the volume slightly.

This was a ruse he used whenever he was going out to make it seem that someone was home. A neighbor's apartment had recently been burgled.

"Hold down the fort, Mitts. Be back later."

~ ~ ~

Jack walked slowly across the tarmac to the arrival gate at Key West International Airport. The balmy evening felt good.

He'd halfway hoped something might've been settled by his making the trip. A reconciliation of sorts. What had he been thinking? At least he was moving on. Progress of a kind. Still, what the hell.

He grabbed a cab outside the terminal. Passing the White Street pier, he had a change of mind about going to his condo.

"Driver, drop me off at the corner of Duval and Truman."

It was a nice night and he was glad to be back in Key West. A walk around town would be fun. Especially since he was wearing a suit. Not the usual dress code for the island. Might raise a few eyebrows. He was smiling at the thought of that when he remembered that he had never asked how his mother had died. Cancer? Broken heart? What a good son.

"This okay?" the driver asked, pulling to the curb just before Truman.

Jack told him it was fine, tipped five bucks on the fare and jumped out. The cab continued down Duval and Jack decided it was as good a direction as any and followed.

A couple of female impersonators, resplendent in drag, stood on the sidewalk outside of Aqua handing out cards for the next show, the bar inside already in full swing.

"Nice suit," one said with a wink as Jack passed.

He walked another block before crossing the street and heading back uptown. He was beginning to feel a little self-conscious about the damn suit. He cut over to Thomas Street and didn't see another soul the whole way back to Truman Annex and Porter Court. There were no lights on in the condo across from him either.

Had Jack continued up Duval until he'd come to Vinos, he would've spotted Earl Gleason.

~ ~ ~

"Another?" the bartender asked.

"Yeah, I'll take it out on the porch,'" Gleason told him.

He settled in an empty chair and checked his phone. Scrolling down its directory he found the number he wanted and punched it in.

"Conch Detective Agency," a sweet voice answered. "This is Alice Devereux."

That she'd picked up the phone herself caught him by surprise. He'd expected to get the answering machine. He hesitated.

"You've got about one more second to say something before I hang up, buster!" Alice warned, all the charm gone.

"This is Earl Gleason, KWPD. Wonder if we could meet tomorrow?"

"We're on the phone now, darling. Talk to me."

Gleason really didn't want to do this over the telephone while sitting on the front porch of Vinos for all the world to listen in. It was bad enough he'd been put in this ridiculous position where he had to involve her in the first place. But here he was, nonetheless. And he did have to admit she was good at what she did.

"I want to hire you," he said.

"Oops ... something caught in the wringer with our boys in blue?"

"Not for me," Gleason huffed. "Another person. You interested or not?"

"I'd need details first."

"Can't say anything here. Too public. When are you free?"

"I'm never free, baby. I can fit you in tomorrow around ten. Since you're so worried about your fans spotting you, you know where I live."

"I'll be there at ten."

Gleason felt relieved after hanging up. Who knows? Maybe there was something fishy going on in Bradenton. Or maybe not. Hiring a private detective to investigate would at least placate his sister and more importantly, get her off his back.

He ordered another glass of merlot.

CHAPTER 7

JACK HAD GOTTEN UP A LITTLE LATER than
usual, the events of the day before having taken more
out of him than he'd realized. He'd showered, dressed
and was just about to step outside when he saw Monica
Kuun leaving her house carrying a large plastic garbage
bag. Probably taking it to the dumpster, which
reminded him that his own kitchen trash can was
overflowing.

~ ~ ~

Detective Powers had faxed a copy of Charles
Gibbs' driver's license photo to the New Bern PD. That
was the protocol most departments followed in such
cases where a victim was from out-of-state. To
ascertain identification. Make sure he was who he was
said to be and not a lookalike or using stolen ID. KWPD
also wanted to learn if there was anything about the
man they needed to know. Was he a drug dealer, for
instance? Wanted for a serious crime? Nothing came
back on Gibbs. Just a local kid from a small town.

The New Bern police volunteered to notify the
victim's parents. And Powers had afterwards made a
sad follow-up call. The boy's father told her that his son
had recently graduated from college and had gone to
Key West with some friends to celebrate. Mr. Gibbs
didn't know what he was supposed to do about getting
his son back home. Powers promised she would help
with that.

"So as soon as the medical examiner releases him,
I'll get on it," she said, finishing updating Gleason.
"Funny, I'd never thought about that. You know,
returning the body."

33

Gleason had come in while she still was on the line. He seemed distracted.

"Tell him to make arrangements with whatever funeral home he wants to use there," he said, sneaking a peek at his watch. "They can coordinate with a mortuary here to have his kid picked up and transported back. What about the suspect?"

"Mr. Malloy is currently enjoying the comforts of county jail on Stock Island, sir. Doesn't want to talk without a lawyer being present. Should we try to interview him anyway?"

"Waste of time," Gleason shrugged. "Make sure your report is tight. Get all the witnesses, details, photos, those good things. You know the drill. I'll see you later."

Powers gave him a puzzled look as he left the detectives' room.

Gleason got in his car but hesitated before putting the key in the ignition. There'd been no reason for his abrupt behavior just now. He'd been rude and unprofessional. He ought to go back inside and apologize to Powers. He checked his watch again. It was nearly ten. He started the engine and drove away. He had gone only one block when his cellphone sang. It was riding in the passenger seat. He reached across and turned it on speaker.

"This is Gleason," he barked.

"Good morning, detective, Blake Hardy here. Just had an odd request thought you might be interesting in knowing about."

Last person he wanted to hear from now.

"Doc, I'm driving down White Street. Shouldn't be on the phone."

"It concerns the Dewitt Pittman autopsy."

"Call Detective Powers. She's at the station. Goodbye."

There he went again, he thought, rude as ever. He switched off the phone and tucked it in his pocket.

Gecko Lane was no more than a short alley, not even paved, but an address you'd have to cough up a fortune to have. Alice's tiny house hid behind a bamboo hedge half way down the lane, a patch of brick courtyard fronting it.

"Almost on time," she greeted from the door as Gleason opened the wrought-iron gate.

"Trouble finding a parking space," he grumbled.

"Come in," Alice said.

The house was a small, wooden-framed two-story box. Downstairs consisted of one large room with a kitchenette and bath at the rear. A narrow stairway against the wall led upstairs to a sleeping loft and a second bath. A tiny balcony opened off that. It was an endearing little place and offered all the room one person could want. Alice had kept the furnishings simple and tasteful.

"Sit anywhere as long as it's in that chair, detective," she gestured at a seating arrangement comprising a matching leather sofa and single chair around a low table. "Coffee?"

Gleason said that coffee would be fine and settled himself in the assigned chair.

"So, what's new in the murder trade?" Alice said from the kitchen. "You want cream?"

"Yes, but no sugar," Gleason said. "Not much is new. Got another detective. Rachel Powers. She's ex-military."

"I saw her name mentioned in the paper during those homeless killings. She's been with the department for a while now, hasn't she?"

Alice placed the two cups of coffee on the table and took a seat.

"Yeah, come to think of it, I guess she has," Gleason sighed. "Time gets away from you."

"How are you doing, Earl?"

She'd picked up on the edginess in his voice.

"Me? Couldn't be better."

"Uh-huh, so what's this all about then? You sounded like it was urgent that we get together. So talk to me."

Gleason laid out the situation with his brother-in-law in Bradenton. And that he'd spoken with the investigating detective there.

"It kind of pisses me off," he said when he'd finished. "My sister's husband supposedly being a drug dealer."

"Why is that? Doesn't reflect anything on you."

Gleason laughed sarcastically.

"That's what Lundy said. Sure. That and a couple of bucks will buy you a cup of coffee."

"He's the detective in Bradenton, right?"

"Bill Lundy. Lead investigator on Frank. A blowhard in my opinion."

Alice sipped her coffee.

"Why do you say that?" she asked.

"I'd mentioned that I felt sort of embarrassed about Frank's being arrested when I called. He started in telling me about his own family. According to him, half the prison population in Florida is named Lundy. Can't tell me that doesn't bother him. Just putting on an act when he pretends otherwise."

Alice smiled.

"Maybe he was just trying to be helpful," she suggested. "Make you feel not all alone."

"Yeah, maybe he was. He dropped the sympathy act when I tried to press him for information."

"Wouldn't you have done that in the same situation?"

"Possibly. But I wasn't asking for what they had on Frank. Evidence to back it up, that sort of stuff. Just where things stood so I could explain to my sister what they're up against. Hell, I've cooperated with other departments. Professional courtesy. No, it was Lundy's sudden shift that didn't set right. I mean this guy has already convicted the man. Then there's the new lawyer. Right away he suggests they make a plea deal. At first I didn't want to get involved with this. My sister and I have been estranged for some time. That's another story. But I'm beginning to think they might have reason to be worried. Something's going on."

Alice leaned back and crossed her arms.

"Alright," she said. "I'll see what I can find out. But your sister will have to realize that her husband could actually be guilty, no matter what she believes now. That detective in Bradenton might be right on the money when he says the man's dirty. I can't promise you otherwise. It could turn out badly."

"I'm okay with that so long as everything's on the up and up. Suppose this would be a good time to discuss your rate."

"You can't afford my rate, baby. But don't worry, I'll give you a discount. Call it professional courtesy."

CHAPTER 8

DETECTIVE POWERS HAD RE-WRITTEN her latest report on the Gibbs homicide. She'd decided to make the do-over since Gleason had suggested she 'tighten' it, whatever that meant. He'd been in a peculiar mood lately. Anyway, she was satisfied with the thing, had made herself a cup of coffee, and was now enjoying it during a rare quiet moment at her desk when the phone rang.

"Homicide. This is Detective Powers."

"Good morning, detective. This is Dr. Hardy. I have something concerning a pending autopsy. You have a moment?"

"I'm all ears, sir."

"I'd spoken earlier with Gleason about this. He seemed interested at the time. But when I called him a little while ago with additional information he appeared to be in a hurry. Couldn't talk."

"Yes, sir," Powers said. "Detective Gleason is busy with another matter."

"I understand. Well, here's the situation. I have an elderly man in the morgue, apparent heart failure, scheduled for autopsy in the next few days and now the man's lawyer is making a stink. Some guy in Baton Rouge, Louisiana. Says the family doesn't want an autopsy. Adamant about it. That's what I wanted to tell Gleason."

"Can the lawyer do that? Prevent an autopsy?"

"No, not really. The state law is clear on autopsies but our office is always open for discussion. We try to accommodate the family's wishes, up to a point."

"Who's the autopsy for?"

"Dewitt Pittway. According to the hospital's admittance information he lived in Louisiana and was in Key West on vacation with his fiancée. The reason I'm involved is the man appears to have been in good health, though he did have a pacemaker. If it's related to the cause of death, then he didn't die of natural causes and we need to know that. I've gone over all of this with Gleason."

"Yes, sir, but thank you for explaining everything to me. Is there anything I can do from our end? Do you have the lawyer's name? Not that it matters, just curious."

"Burton Sachs. Reminds me of anatomy."

"Sir?"

"As in bursa sac. It's a little membrane filled with fluid that cushions your bone joints, say around the hips. A bruised bursa sac can be a real pain in the ass."

"I'll take your word for that," Powers laughed. "Again, I'd be happy to help, although I don't know what I can do about the bruised attorney."

"It would be helpful for me to have Pittway's medical history," Hardy said. "Lawyer's fighting that, too. Whole thing's kind of odd. I thought Gleason could talk with the lady, explain the situation."

"Perhaps that's something I can do."

~ ~ ~

"You can enjoy the sunsets without setting a foot on Mallory Square," the real estate agent smiled.

Jack looked out the west-facing window in the living room. Two cruise ships blocked most of the view. What little remained was of an approaching storm.

"It's not always like that," the agent said, noticing the ships.

"Yeah, well, I'm not all that into sunsets anyway. Don't worry. I still like the place."

The agent relaxed.

"We can go back to the office and get the paperwork started," he suggested.

"Give me a couple more days to think about it," Jack told him.

"Sure, Mr. Hunter. Only thing is, condos like this in Harbour Place don't come up all that often. I'd hate to see you miss out."

"I appreciate your concern," Jack said. "I'd still like a couple of days, okay?"

Jack said goodbye to the agent, and seeing that it was nearly lunch time, walked down Front Street to the Pier House. A few raindrops were beginning to fall. He picked up his pace and made it to the restaurant just as a rumble of thunder shook loose a cloudburst. Seating himself at the bar, he noticed Alice alone at a table.

"Mind if I join you?" he said, going over to her.

"For you, anytime you want, sweetie," she said saucily.

Alice had already ordered her favorite dish, shrimp salad, and Jack told the waiter he'd have the same.

"How's that lovely lady in Los Angeles?" she asked.

"Laura Dalton? She's fine, I guess."

Alice pursed her lips.

"Uh, oh, something going on I should know about?"

Jack felt himself blush and the goofy grin crept up his face.

"We've had a meeting of the minds," he said.

Alice leaned back in her chair and gave him a look.

"What's that supposed to mean? Meeting of the minds?"

"Just that we both realized that our relationship had stalled. Wasn't going anywhere. Stepping back was her idea, actually."

"Do I sense disappointment here?"

Jack smiled.

"A little, to be honest. But she was right and I accept that now. We're still friends. Best of friends."

Alice smiled sympathetically.

"I'm sorry, Jack. But maybe this was inevitable. I could tell there was a spark between the two of you the first time we all met. But sometimes that spark never bursts into a real flame. She and I write to each other occasionally. Did she ever tell you?"

This was unexpected news to Jack.

"I'm sort of the go-between her and her brother. He moved back to New York from Brazil. No longer Charlize, the hot fashion model in Rio, now just plain Charles on Seventh Avenue. Decided not to go through with the gender reassignment. Good decision. Like I suspected, the boy isn't transgender. He's gay. I stay in touch with him, too, and keep Laura updated. Can't understand why there's still this riff between them. Families are funny."

Jack could tell her something about families. His shrimp salad arrived.

"These shrimp are fresh today," Alice commented. "Dig in."

They both remained silent for a few minutes, enjoying their lunch.

"So what's up with you other than mending a broken heart?" Alice asked.

"Thinking of buying a condo at Harbour Place. Not sure about it, though."

"Very, very upscale is all I know," Alice said, munching a shrimp. "Personally, I wouldn't be happy there. No reflection on the place, however. Just not me."

"Could turn out not me, either. Haven't made a final decision. Right now, I'm not sure about Truman Annex period. Man across from where I'm renting in

Porter Court had a heart attack and died. I was talking with Earl Gleason about it."

"Isn't that a coincidence? Gleason and I just had a chat ourselves this morning. But what was the deal with your neighbor that you had to talk with him about? Heart attack happens every day to someone."

"He was an older guy. Died in bed. His girlfriend came outside screaming for help. I went in and began CPR. I could tell he was already gone but still, you know? She was worried about the autopsy so I called Earl to try to get some info."

"What about the EMTs when they arrived?"

"The medics were afraid to use a defibrillator because he had a pacemaker. But like I said, the poor fellow was long gone."

"Luck of the draw, I guess."

~ ~ ~

"Thank you for your time, Miss Kuun," Powers said, brushing the rain from her jacket. "The storm caught me by surprise. I didn't have an umbrella."

Monica Kuun smiled politely.

"I hope this won't take too long," she said. "I have an appointment."

"I promise to be brief."

Powers had called her, having finally found her cellphone number on the original police report. No matter how much she'd browbeaten the hospital admissions office for the number, they wouldn't budge. Patient privacy issue.

"I wasn't expecting a call on my phone from the police," Monica said. "I found it frightening, to tell you the truth."

"Just routine, ma'am," Powers said.

"I don't understand why the police are involved," Monica continued. "Dewitt had a heart attack. Didn't the hospital tell you? I'd think you would have real crimes to solve."

"Again, just a routine follow-up," Powers told her. "Something we have to do."

"If you say so."

"This is a lovely condo," Powers commented, seating herself on a sofa. "So fresh and everything. Truman Annex is a beautiful area."

"I suppose so," Monica replied, "but it doesn't seem lovely to me. And if it seems fresh, it's because I had the maid service scrub down everything. I'm sure you can understand why. Still, I'm looking for another place to stay until this problem with the hospital is handled and I can get Dewitt home."

"Of course. And I am sorry for your loss. Had you and Mr. Pittway known one another for long?"

"Not very long. But we were engaged."

"How did you meet? Were you neighbors?"

"We first met in New Orleans. He came there often on business. We were introduced by a mutual friend. We started going out and it just went from there."

"Love at first sight?" Powers teased girlishly.

"Maybe second," Monica smiled.

"Obviously there was a big difference in age between the two of you. Did that matter?"

"No, I was interested in the man, not his birthdays."

"Aside from Mr. Pittway's heart problem, did his age restrict him in anyway?"

"What? Because he was old, you think he couldn't get it up?"

"I don't mean to offend, just trying to put together a picture of him," Powers said. "Again, this is just routine and I realize our meeting this way must be difficult for you."

Monica welled up a tear.

"He was the most wonderful, generous person in the world," she said, dabbing at her eye. "You wouldn't find a kinder man than Dewitt. Everyone loved him."

"Had he been married before? Does he have a family?"

"There are three children from two previous marriages. Two boys and a girl. Well, they're adults now and have their own families, of course."

"They all live in Louisiana?"

"His sons are both in Cleopus. That's in St. Julian Parish. Dewitt's people have been there for ages. He and I live in the old family house. The daughter lives somewhere else in another state. She's the oldest and from his first marriage."

"How did they feel about you and Dewitt? Was there any resentment?"

"Why would there have been?"

"Just that sometimes children have problems about a parent marrying someone else."

"Dewitt's children didn't. Their father and I loved each other. That's what matters. Besides, they had been through that before, hadn't they?"

"I suppose you could say that," Powers smiled. "But tell me this, was his personal doctor also there in Cleopus? The reason I'm asking is it would help our medical examiner here with his investigation if he could talk with Mr. Pittway's physician. Perhaps even speed things up for you."

Monica paused before answering.

"Do you mean then they wouldn't have to do the autopsy?" she asked.

"Having his medical record would certainly go a long way toward closing the investigation."

Monica gave that another moment of thought.

"His doctor is in Baton Rouge," she said at last. "I don't have his name but I can get it. The family doesn't want an autopsy."

"I'm sure the doctor here will respect that," Powers said, getting to her feet. "I believe we're finished. Thank you for your time."

Monica led her to the door.

"Oh, may I ask what kind of work did you do, Miss Kuun?"

"Why is that important?" Monica asked.

"Just curious. You said that you and Mr. Pittway met in New Orleans. Were you in business there?"

"I was a fashion model."

"Yes, I can see that," Powers smiled, handing her a business card. "Don't forget to call me with the doctor's name."

~ ~ ~

Front Street was ankle-deep in water on the sidewalks. Step off the curb and you were up to your knees. Jack, shoes in hand, had waded across a flooded Duval where a pickup truck was pulling a guy on a surfboard toward Sloppy Joes. Overhead the sky had cleared and the sun beamed as if nothing had happened. He padded barefoot to Truman Annex and higher ground.

Monica Kuun was standing at the window talking on her phone when Jack entered the compound. She stepped back out of view.

"The nosy neighbor just came in," she said. "He looks soaking wet."

"Never mind him," Burton Sachs snapped. "Get back to the detective."

"She wants to look at Dewitt's medical record."

"I've talked to their medical examiner there. Don't worry about it."

"Well, I *am* worried. Suppose they suspect something?"

"I'll get the damn medical records to them. Nothing to suspect—the records will prove that. Now, that make you feel better?"

Monica took a breath and let it out.

"How much longer do I have to stay in this condo?" she said anxiously. "It's creepy. I want to move somewhere else."

"You can't leave there until everything is settled. Shouldn't be much longer. Now stop worrying. You're starting to make *me* nervous."

"Oh, *I'm* making *you* nervous? How do you think I feel? This wasn't the way it was supposed to be, Burton. Nothing could go wrong, remember? Now the police are sniffing around. Somebody better start worrying. In fact, I don't want anything more to do with the whole business. This was a stupid idea in the first place. So find me another place or I'm out of here. Don't fuck with me, Burton. I mean it!"

"Stay cool, Monica. I've got it handled."

Sachs hung up before she could say anymore. The medical record wasn't a problem. But Monica was starting to become a *big* problem.

CHAPTER 9

GLEASON HAD GRABBED A SANDWICH at Fausto's and was eating it at his desk when Powers came into the detectives' room.

"Reminds me, I haven't had lunch," she said.

"Take the other half," Gleason offered. "I haven't touched it."

"Thanks, sir, but think I'll pass. Still have a couple of pounds to lose."

"Suit yourself," Gleason shrugged. "Pretty good roast beef you're missing."

"I just had an interesting talk with the Kuun woman."

"The who?"

"Monica Kuun. She's the girlfriend of Dewitt Pittway."

"Oh, yeah. How's that coming?"

There was that distracted behavior again, Powers thought. Should she say something about it to him?

"After you left this morning, Dr. Hardy called me," Powers said. "He'd tried reaching you but you were busy on another matter. Anyway, we spoke about the autopsy he was to perform on Mr. Pittway. Apparently, the deceased's attorney has gotten in the picture. Hardy wants Pittway's medical records. The doctor thought you should talk with Monica Kuun. Since you weren't available, I volunteered. Hope I didn't step out of line, sir."

Gleason pursed his lips and nodded.

"Not out of line at all, Rachel. What's your take on the girlfriend?"

"She's attractive, not all that forthcoming. Seems a little on edge. Could attribute that to waking up in bed with a dead man. Very concerned about the autopsy. Trotted out the lawyer. I didn't mention we already knew about him, not that it mattered."

"Did she say how they met? I understand her boyfriend was old enough to have been her granddad."

"Matchmaker in New Orleans. Love at second sight. According to her, Pittway is old Louisiana stock. Lawyer probably handles the family business, whatever that is."

"Let's go see the Lieutenant."

~ ~ ~

Jack had decided to walk to the Inedible Cafe rather than ride his scooter. Many of the streets were still flooded but the sidewalks had begun to surface. He saw Billy standing by a stack of sandbags blocking the front door.

"Little sprinkle comes along and the damn street thinks it's a river," Billy groused. "Good thing I keep a few of these bags handy."

"Maybe the city should clean the drains," Jack said.

"Whole damn island's stopped-up, Jack. City can't do nothing. Bring those bags around back and let's have a cup of coffee."

There were eight heavy bags and it took four trips before Jack had finished the job. A freshly brewed pot waited in the kitchen.

"Why don't you get a hand truck, Billy?" Jack asked, pulling out a chair. "Make life a lot easier."

"Already got enough junk in here. Can't keep anything in the alley. Somebody'd steal it. So what's up, Jack? Sorry about your momma. Did she have a good funeral?"

Jack hadn't seen Billy since returning from New Jersey.

"I missed the graveside service," he said, trying to imagine what a *good* funeral might be. "Limo driver got lost. But I was able to talk with my uncle. He was still there."

"I read somewhere about this fellow who does funerals," Billy said. "Folks come to him when they want something done that's out of the box. Pretty funny, huh? Out of the box, hee-hee."

Jack wondered what was coming next.

"He did a special funeral for this lady who'd loved watching football games. Season couldn't come fast enough or last long enough for her, hee-hee. Always watching football games. So when she passed, family called him. Wanting something special for the lady, you see. The fellow thought about it and came up with an idea. He sat her in a chair around a table full of little football helmets. Stuck a beer in one hand and a cigarette in the other, same as she'd been doing all her life."

Jack had no trouble picturing the scene. Where did he get this stuff?

"Story said the whole business of throwing crazy funerals started when this one funeral parlor turned a viewing room into a boxing ring for a prize fighter who'd died. Dressed him in a pair of trunks, put on a pair of boxing gloves, and propped him up in a corner like he was waiting for the next round, hee-hee."

"My uncle always said a little humor takes the edge off anything."

"Your uncle got that right, Jack. By the way, that new band's playing here tonight. Thought you might want to come."

"What's its name again?"

"Torment."

~ ~ ~

Gleason and Powers were seated in Jay Halderman's office. The two detectives had just updated the lieutenant on the latest twist in the Pittway autopsy.

"The medical examiner's office is usually sympathetic when it comes to respecting a family's wishes," Halderman said.

Gleason gave Powers a sideways glance.

"Wait a minute," Gleason broke in. "Are you telling me they can stop the autopsy? I thought there was a law about that."

"There *is* a law. All I'm saying is that the ME will acknowledge their concerns. Settle down, Earl."

"Blake Hardy called us," Gleason said. "Suspicious about the heart attack. Guy had a pacemaker. That's all *I'm* saying."

"The lawyer seems to be throwing up roadblocks," Powers added. "Holding back medical records. Makes you wonder why. Also, something about the girlfriend. Seems more nervous than distraught. I'd like to run her down with New Orleans police."

"Was Pittway from there?" Gleason asked, turning to Powers. "Lived in New Orleans?"

"No, he was from some other place," she said, taking out a note pad. "Here it is. Cleopus. The girlfriend said it was in St. Julian Parish, wherever that is. Also told me his doctor's office is in Baton Rouge. Lawyer's there, too."

"Never heard of Cleopus," Gleason said. "Doubt if there are many heart specialists around there. Lawyers, either. Might be a good idea for Detective Powers to check out the local department in that parish. What do you think, Lieutenant?"

Powers looked askance at Gleason.

"Give 'em a call," Halderman said, reaching for a stack of papers. "Keep me posted."

The two detectives returned to their desks.

"Let me get us a couple coffees, sir," Powers said. "I'd like to go over something with you."

Gleason nodded and sat down.

"Cream, no sugar," she smiled, returning and placing a cup on his desk.

She leaned across and spoke quietly.

"Sir, and again I don't mean to step out of line, but you haven't been yourself lately. I'm a good listener if you'd like to share."

Gleason sipped his coffee.

"That obvious, huh?"

"Only to me."

He sat a moment longer without speaking.

"Family matter," he said. "Involves my sister and her husband. Nothing to do with the department. Nor with me."

"I understand. However, if there's anything I can do for you, I'd be only too happy. You know that."

"Yes, I do know and thank you, Rachel. It's a little embarrassing, that's all. Thanks again. I'm taking care of it."

"All right, sir. Just so you know what other people do isn't about you. Not one iota."

"You aren't the first one to tell me that."

The desk officer came into the detectives' room.

"Detective Gleason," he called out. "Man named Judd Pittway is out front. Says he needs to talk with whoever's investigating his dad's death."

~ ~ ~

Monica had seen Jack leave his condo. She waited a minute and then followed, keeping on the opposite side of the street and lagging a half block behind.

They exited the main gate and continued up Thomas until Jack cut over to avoid a few streets that were still flooded. He stopped at a restaurant where a small black man stood by the front door barricaded with sandbags. She hung back out of sight. Jack seemed to know him and they talked for a few seconds. The man left and Jack began carrying the sandbags around to the rear of the building. She waited a few minutes after he'd finished and then walked quickly past the restaurant herself, turning to read its sign. The Inedible Cafe. About as dumb as the rest of this town, she thought.

~ ~ ~

Judd Pittway was medium height, average build, looked to be in his mid-thirties and wore his black hair slicked back. He had on a pair of expensive cowboy boots, designer jeans and a golf shirt. He sat at the end of a table in an interview room at the KWPD station with Gleason.

"This where you bring the suspects?" he grinned, looking around. "Don't see any rubber hoses."

"It's a good place to come for privacy," Gleason said, ignoring the tired joke. "Sometimes it can get pretty hectic out there."

Powers entered the room carrying two cups of coffee and a bottle of water. She handed Pittway the water and placed one cup on the table in front Gleason, then seated herself next to him.

"First, we're sorry about your father," Gleason began. "However, I'm not sure how we can help you with anything since he apparently died from natural causes. At least that's where things stand at the moment. Do you have reason to suspect differently?"

Judd screwed off the bottle cap and took a drink.

"My dad was in good health last time I saw him," he said. "Getting a little forgetful but otherwise healthy as a horse. I'm here because of his latest girlfriend. I don't like her and the feeling is mutual. Mainly, I don't trust her."

"I assume you're talking about Monica Kuun," Gleason said. "We've spoken with her."

"Did she use that phony French accent?" Judd laughed. "It was a turn-on for dad. She's pretty clever that way."

"I don't believe I noticed any accent," Powers said.

"Detective Powers interviewed Ms. Kuun," Gleason explained.

"Why don't you trust her?" Powers asked. "I can understand not liking someone but what has she done to make you not trust her?"

"She has an agenda."

"Could you expand on that?" Gleason asked.

"Okay, a little history first. My dad is seventy years old and has chased women since I can remember. Wyatt and I just shrug our shoulders when another one turns up. Dad being dad, no big deal. He wasn't going to change so why get up tight about it? But Renee couldn't take it. She moved out."

Renee? Wyatt?" Powers smiled curiously.

"Renee's my stepsister from dad's first marriage. She lives in California with her own family. She's estranged from the Pittways. Wyatt's my brother. Dad divorced our mom some years back. Then married again. Divorced. Married. Divorced. Like I said, we were used to his gallivanting. Girlfriends came and they went. But Monica was different. She knew how to play him. Even her last name worked in her favor."

"Excuse me?" Powers said.

"Double letters," Judd laughed. "Started 'way back when. Like dad is Dewitt with a double *t*. Same for Wyatt. I'm Judd with two *d*'s. Renee back-to-back *e*'s. And wouldn't you just know it? Along comes Kuun. Two damn *u*'s stuck together in the middle. Dad even checked our family history to see if she was any kind of relation."

"Back to the agenda you mentioned," Gleason said. "What was it about?"

"Worming her way into the family so she could get ahold of his money."

"How was she going to do that? There'd been a long line of girlfriends. How was she any different?"

"Number one, she moved into the family house," Judd stated, lifting a finger. "That's never happened before. Dad always kept his playmates at a distance. Although he and Monica did have separate bedrooms for whatever that matters."

"Not a crime, yet," Gleason said.

"Next thing, she's talking marriage big time" Judd told him, raising a second finger. "Pressing dad for an engagement ring. He always shines them off when they get pushy. But not this time. So there's that."

"Still no law broken," Gleason said, "unless things are different in Louisiana."

"Number three," Judd said, another finger joining the pair. "Sat in on family business meetings. Hadn't been there a week before that started."

"Your dad was all right with this?" Powers asked. "Marriage and the meetings? Did you and your brother tell him your concerns?"

"He'd always listen to you but he'd already made up his mind."

"What I'm hearing here may be untoward but so far nothing unlawful," Gleason said. "Sounds to me like the right person came along and he fell in love. Happens."

"The right person?" Judd laughed. "Here's how he met Miss Right. The law firm that handles our business is in Baton Rouge. This one lawyer there is an asshole. Never liked him. Grew up near us. He was a big jock in school. My dad did some business with his old man. Didn't work out but that's another story. Anyway, my dad starts partying with him. Mostly they'd go to New Orleans. That's where he hooked up with Monica."

"Ms. Kuun is a fashion model, I understand," Powers said. "Her agency is in New Orleans?"

"Try escort service," Judd smirked.

"Not all escort services are illegitimate," Powers said. "Some provide companions for, say, important social events."

"You don't know Monica," Judd smirked again.

"I still don't see anything suspicious even given that," Gleason said. "If she and your father were planning to marry, then naturally she would want to know about what he does."

"Normally I'd agree," Judd nodded, "but check this. The lawyer sent a big envelope full of papers the other day addressed to dad. I asked him about it and he said it was something he had to sign. He took it back to the post office himself. Wyatt always takes the mail there."

"Could be he just wanted to stretch his legs," Gleason said.

"Uh-huh, and I could go along with that, too, except Wyatt and I work for my dad. We're land developers. So wouldn't you think anything coming from the lawyer that needed a signature would've involved us?"

"Maybe it was a life insurance policy," Gleason suggested. "Wanted to add his fiancée to it."

"Dad didn't believe in life insurance. Said it was a waste of money."

"So what do you think they were?" Gleason asked. "These mysterious papers?"

"I don't know. That's what worries me."

"Why did your dad come to Key West?" Powers asked.

"Oh, he has been here many times," Judd said. "Brought Wyatt and me once when we were younger."

"Did he always stay at Porter Court?"

"Porter Court? Never heard of it. No, Dad rented a private house then. What's Porter Court?"

"It's a condominium community in Truman Annex. He and Ms. Kuun were staying there."

Judd shook his head.

"Must've been her idea," he said. "One more thing she stuck her nose in."

"How long are you going to be in town, Mr. Pittway?" Powers asked.

"I'll fly back tomorrow morning. The airplane has a charter scheduled the next day. My hotel here's near the airport. Plan to get an early start providing the weather cooperates."

"Business must be good for you to take a charter flight," Gleason said.

"We own the airplane," Judd told him. "It's a new Piper M600. I'm also a pilot and flew it down myself. We use the plane in business. Saves a lot of time and expense getting around the state. We also lease the plane to a charter company at Baton Rouge Metropolitan. Helps with taxes. In fact, one of their pilots brought dad and Monica here. I wouldn't fly them. Too pissed off about Monica. Told 'em to get Bruce Mason. He's a pilot for the charter outfit, Eborn Jet Center there at the airport."

"You said your dad was in good health," Powers said, "yet he suffered from a heart problem. Was it severe?"

"No, he had an irregular heartbeat and a year or so ago started feeling a little weak. Couple of dizzy spells. His doctor had him get a pacemaker and that took care of it. Been good as new ever since."

"The medical examiner is curious about that," Gleason said. "He wants to perform an autopsy."

"Why do they need to do one of those? The lawyer didn't say anything about an autopsy when he called to tell us dad had died."

Gleason looked at Powers.

"Ms. Kuun didn't notify you herself?" he asked.

Judd shook his head.

"Guess she felt better letting the lawyer handle it. Like I said, no love lost between us. Even less now."

Powers jotted down a note.

"The autopsy would confirm what caused his heart to fail," Gleason explained. "If the pacemaker was at fault or by some other means. It's important to know. Especially in light of what you just said about his being so healthy after the procedure. Would you have a problem with the autopsy?"

Judd considered that for a moment.

"Kind of gruesome thing to think about when it's your own dad but I guess not," he said.

"Well, here's where the situation stands at present," Gleason said. "Ms. Kuun insists that your dad did not want to have an autopsy. Were you aware of his feelings in that regard? Or are there any religious reasons he might've had not to want one?"

"Nope, never heard him say anything one way or the other. Not exactly a topic we talk about around the dinner table. And as far as religion goes, that's not a big subject with us, either."

"The medical examiner always listens to the family's wishes and tries to abide by them," Gleason said, "but he has the last say. If he deems an autopsy to be necessary, then it'll be done. He will be respectful of your father."

"Thanks, detective, but I doubt if my dad will know. When do you think the autopsy will be done?"

"Probably in the next few days."

"Will you see Ms. Kuun before you leave?" Powers asked.

"Not if I can help it."

CHAPTER 10

JACK FELT GOOD. He'd just gotten off the phone with Ruby Steele and had invited her to Torment's opening night at the Inedible Cafe. The two of them shared a love of music. Ruby had been a rock-and roll-sensation in Miami at one time. She'd been living with Jewel Banks on a sailboat in Garrison Bight after returning to Key West but had moved to an apartment. He liked Ruby. They'd been casual friends once before. He hoped to renew that relationship. Could even see the possibility of it becoming something more serious. He wouldn't mind.

There was a knock at the door. He snuck a peek out the window. Monica stood waiting.

"Hello, Jack, may I come in for a moment?"

He ushered her to a seat on the sofa.

"Could I get you something?" he asked.

"That's kind of you but I'm fine."

Jack took a seat in a chair to the side.

"How are you doing?"

"Not well. There is still a problem with the medical people."

"I'm sorry."

"On second thought, I will have something to drink, if you don't mind. Perhaps a glass of wine?"

Jack went into the kitchen.

"Chablis okay?" he called.

"Perfect."

He returned with a single glass.

"Aren't you joining me?"

"I have an engagement later."

"Oh," she smiled. "I hope I'm not keeping you."

"Not at all."

"I was out for a walk today and saw you," she said.

"Really, where was that?"

"Not too far from here. You were at a restaurant talking with a man. Is he a friend?"

For some reason, Jack began to feel slightly uneasy.

"We've known each other for some time," he said.

"Have you eaten at that restaurant? How is it?"

"It's very good. Although the name might put some people off."

"Why is that?"

"It's called the Inedible Cafe," Jack laughed.

"I think it's charming," Monica laughed back. "Perhaps you'll take me there? Tonight?"

"I really can't tonight. But another time, sure."

"I understand," Monica said disappointedly.

She took a sip of wine, giving a slightly seductive glance over the glass at Jack.

"Jack, I'd like to stay here. Could I? Not for long, just a couple of nights. I might be leaving Key West after that. No one would even know I was here."

Jack was taken aback by her forwardness.

"I can't stand it over there any longer," she gestured to her condo. "The whole place creeps me out. Would you mind?"

Jack did mind.

"Tell you what, I know a real estate agent who handles properties in the Annex. His office is right here. They do short-term rentals. Could move you to a vacant one. I'll call him now."

"No, not now," she said, standing. "Thank you for the wine, Jack."

"I'll call him anyway," he said. "Find out what's available."

He watched as she walked back to her condo. He felt sorry for her. What would it matter if she spent a few nights here? There was plenty of room. He picked up his phone and dialed the real estate agent. The voice mail answered. Checking his watch, he saw that he had only an hour before he was to meet Ruby. He'd better get dressed.

Monica was presently rummaging through the closet in her bedroom. She decided on the cute little form-fitting frock and placed it on the bed. An evening out anywhere was better than being alone in this gloomy place. She went to take a shower.

~ ~ ~

Torment wasn't bad providing you were into cool jazz. A lot of Miles Davis in their first set, which Jack had loved but he sensed that Ruby had sided with the bandleader's daughter. On the possibility – make that a sure bet – they'd stick with Miles after their break, he did the right thing.

"Wanna split?" he asked.

"Oh, aren't they coming back for another set?" Ruby asked.

"I'm good to go if you are."

Jack went to thank the band, stuck a twenty in the tip bowl, and they left.

~ ~ ~

All the chairs were taken on the front porch at Vinos. Gleason found a spot at the bar. He ordered a glass of merlot and looked around the room. Mostly regulars and a few tourists. His eye stopped on an attractive woman seated at the end of the bar, lost in conversation with the man next to her. The guy looked local. He hadn't seen the woman before. Could be someone off the cruise ship. His wine came just as a seat opened on the porch.

"I'll take it outside," he told the bartender.

Much better, Gleason thought, as he settled in the comfortable wicker chair. A small group walked past with nametags pinned on their shirts and carrying rum-filled pineapples. Just as he figured, cruise ship's in port. His cellphone chimed with *I Shot the Sheriff*. The man seated next to him turned and looked disdainfully.

"Hello, Charlotte," Gleason answered, cutting his eyes sharply at the man.

"You didn't say she was black."

"What?"

"You didn't tell me that private detective was going to be a black person. You know how Frank is."

Gleason shook his head wearily. He got up and went to the sidewalk.

"Frank still with the Klan?" he asked, standing at the curb.

"He never was a Ku Kluxer, Earl. Don't try to be funny. It's just I'd like to have known she was black, that's all."

"Well, you might also like to know that Alice is a former police officer and a very good investigator. Frank has a problem with her being black, fine – I'll tell her she's off the case. You can hire someone more to Frank's liking."

"No, don't do that. If you say she's good, then that's all that matters. I'm so scared about what might happen, Earl."

Gleason noticed the woman at the bar coming down the steps. She was even better looking than he'd thought. And that dress she barely had on didn't hurt, either. She flashed him a smile as she passed, the guy she'd been talking with catching up when she'd gotten to the sidewalk. They both continued down Duval.

"It's going to be okay, Charlotte," he said. "Alice will get to the bottom of this. Take care."

He ended the call and returned to his chair on the porch. The one next to it was now vacant.

~ ~ ~

Ruby Steele and Jack stood ninety miles from Cuba at the elbow of Whitehead and South Streets. Tourists flocked here every day to have their picture taken in front of the big yellow, red and black Southernmost Point marker. Some locals made a living taking those photographs for them.

"My apartment's a couple of houses down," Ruby said. "I'd invite you in but the place is a wreck. Still haven't unpacked everything."

"I know how that can be," Jack said with a tinge of disappointment he hoped didn't show.

"It's beautiful here tonight," Ruby said.

"It was a night just like this when I left Key West the first time. Sparrow Lovewell picked me up right at the marker and we drove to Miami. I was running from the law."

"I'd love to hear the rest of that story," Ruby said. "Wanna tell me?"

"But your apartment's a wreck."

"Perhaps we could straighten it up together."

CHAPTER 11

"THANKS FOR SEEING ME, DETECTIVE," Alice said. She and Lundy were at a small restaurant just outside of Bradenton. Alice, having gotten into town the previous night, had called him first thing in the morning and to her surprise he'd agreed to a meeting.

"No problem," Lundy smiled. "Although I'm not sure what I can do for you."

"Tell you the truth, I'm not either," she smiled back. "First, let me show you my PI card."

She handed him her Florida private investigator certificate. He took a quick glance and returned it. The waitress arrived with a couple of menus.

"Coffee?" she asked.

"That'd be great," Lundy told her. "And give us a few minutes before taking our orders, okay?"

She poured two cups and left the table.

"They do a killer poached egg in a fresh croissant, Miss Devereux."

"Alice will do."

"How long were you with the Jacksonville department, Alice?"

"Ten years. Worked patrol the whole time. No reflection on upstairs but I preferred the streets."

She'd mentioned being a former police officer when she had called. Sometimes that greased the skids. Other times not.

"Like I said, I'm investigating a possession-with-intent regarding Frank Anderson. I'm really not all that familiar with the drug scene here other than statistics I can get anywhere. Anything you can share with me from your perspective would be appreciated."

"Bradenton's probably no better or worse than Key West," Lundy said. "We get our share of coke, meth, pills ... who'd you say hired you?"

"I didn't say. That's confidential."

"Key West detective called me about Anderson. Name's Gleason. You know him?"

"As a matter of fact, I do know Detective Gleason."

"I think he has some personality issues," Lundy said

"The rumor is he flunked charm school," Alice laughed, "but Gleason is a good cop. I've worked with him."

"He was trying to pump me for information about the case. His sister's married to Anderson. Claims her hubby's innocent, of course."

The waitress returned. They both ordered the poached egg.

"Well, I'll say this, you do have better manners than he does," he chuckled. "Personally, I think Gleason's more concerned about his reputation. Bothers him that there might be a bad guy in the family. Hell, that happens in the best of them. I tried to tell him that. Got all huffy."

"Will there be anything more?" the waitress asked.

Lundy nodded no.

"So tell me, Alice," he said when she'd left, "are you working for Gleason?"

"I'm here for the family. Saw them last night."

Lundy looked at her, measuring.

"Okay, here's what we have on Anderson," he said. "Word was that stolen motorcycles were supposedly coming into his shop and being repurposed to sell. Fake titles, the works. Got a warrant and paid him a visit. No suspicious bikes found on the premises. But while checking for bogus paperwork, we found a big stash of meth in Anderson's desk."

"That's not much to go on," Alice said. "Anyone could've put it there. Certainly doesn't prove he was dealing drugs."

"We also have a witness."

~ ~ ~

Jack had slept through the Key West reveille. The post office roosters, having other business to attend to, had long moved on and it wasn't until an hour later that he struggled out of bed. His muscles felt a little sore. Ruby Steele had been serious about him helping her straighten the apartment. Afterwards, they'd talked nearly to dawn.

Now he was showered, dressed and enjoying a cup of coffee at poolside. He noticed no activity in the condo across from where he sat. He wondered if Monica had moved after all. He got up from the table and walked over.

"Monica?" he called out at the door. "It's Jack Hunter."

No response. He called again, rapping the door, which swung open, apparently having been left unlatched. He stuck in his head.

"Hello. Anyone home?"

He stepped inside. Nothing appeared to be out of order. She'd probably just forgotten to pull the door shut when she'd gone out, he reasoned. As he turned to leave, a foreboding came over him. Letting the door stand open, he continued through the living room to the kitchen.

"Monica?" he called uncertainly.

He halted abruptly at the kitchen entrance.

There, Monica Kuun lay sprawled on the floor, her cute little frock ripped down the front, her head twisted unnaturally to one side.

CHAPTER 12

PATROL RESPONDED TO THE CALL. The two officers saw Jack waiting and hustled over.

"You phone in the 911, sir?" one of them asked.

"Yeah, I live over there," Jack said, pointing to his condo.

"Okay, stay here with this officer while I take a look."

He went inside and returned a moment later with a grim expression on his face.

"Detective's on the way," he told his partner.

"Do you know the person in there, sir?" he asked Jack.

"Not really. It's a rental. She and her fiancé recently arrived. Older man. Poor guy had a heart attack. Monica found him unconscious. I happened to be out here by the pool and went in to help. Tried CPR but no luck."

"Who's Monica?"

"The dead lady."

"How long did you say they'd been here?" he asked.

"I really haven't been counting. Several days, I don't know exactly."

"Seem to know them pretty well, though."

"It's a small community here," Jack smiled.

"Even smaller now," the cop wise-guyed.

Jack was just opening his mouth to protest when the gate banged open and a man entered dressed in a dark blue suit and wearing a grey fedora with the brim snapped down.

"I'm Detective Sonny Breaks," he announced, holding up a newly-minted badge. "Where's the victim?"

"In there on the kitchen floor, Sonny," the cop said.

Breaks frowned.

"It's *sir* or *detective*, officer," he said, raising his right eyebrow.

Sonny Breaks had a habit of emphasizing with an arched eyebrow.

He pointed to Jack, the eyebrow shooting up again.

"And who are you?"

"Jack Hunter. I'm a neighbor."

"He discovered the body...detective," the officer said.

Breaks stepped up to Jack and looked him squarely in the face.

"You stay here with this man," he indicated to one cop, not taking his eyes off Jack. And to the other officer, "You come with me."

Sonny Breaks had joined KWPD straight out of police academy. He'd spent four years working patrol, during which time he'd earned a strong reputation for mediocrity, but a family member with heavy political connections had shielded him from any reprimand. Upon learning of a possible detective slot opening and feeling his abilities might be better appreciated elsewhere, Sonny had squeaked through the detective tests, and with considerable outside influence, had managed to get himself kicked up to the burglary table.

He'd been the only detective present when the possible homicide call came in at Truman Annex. Since he dealt with felonies and sensing this could be his big case, he'd jumped right on it.

"Nobody goes inside," Breaks shouted in a shaky voice from the front door. "This is now a crime scene. Anyone got yellow tape?"

One cop volunteered he had a roll in the patrol car and went to get it.

Breaks walked over to where Jack waited with the other officer.

"How well did you know the woman in there?" he asked, a squint this time.

"I didn't know her," Jack shrugged. "She and her boyfriend just got here. Didn't know him, either. I explained all that to the officers."

Breaks didn't care for Jack's attitude. He cocked an eyebrow.

"So you just wandered in and found her dead on the floor," he said. "Do you do that often? Barge into stranger's homes unannounced?"

"No, the door was open," Jack said. "She didn't want to stay there any longer because the man she was with had died the night they arrived. I thought she'd moved out."

"Another death? Did you chance upon that body as well?"

"The guy had a heart attack," Jack said. "Monica called me. I tried to help."

"Monica?" Breaks grinned. "You know each other pretty well. How about from before?"

"I've never seen her before in my life. And I resent what you're trying to imply."

"I bet you do. And when was the last time you saw her? Alive, that is."

"Yesterday afternoon. She came over."

"Cozy."

"What does that mean?"

"Did you kill her?"

"No, and before you start asking questions like that aren't you supposed to read me my rights?"

"We'll take care of that at the station," Breaks said, then, turning to the cop, "cuff this man and put him in the car."

~ ~ ~

Gleason and Powers had been tied up in court all morning. The murder trial of Mike Galvin was in its third week. Galvin was charged with committing four homicides in the infamous Blue Bayou murders involving homeless victims. The two detectives were due to testify but the judge had called a recess for the rest of the day.

"Want to grab lunch?" Gleason asked.

He and Powers were driving back to the police station.

"You stop if you want," Powers said. "I'm still trying to lose a few more pounds. Think it'll help my back. Been awful lately."

"Doc at the vets' hospital in Miami couldn't give you anything to help?"

"Yeah, they could've but I'd rather stay clean. Drugs have too many side effects. And there's no way I'd use opioids."

"Any kind of exercise you can do?"

"Walking works best. I've been thinking about trying magnets."

Gleason laughed.

"The little things you stick on the fridge?"

"No, the magnets are in a mattress pad. You sleep on them. Supposed to relieve pain. There's no proof they work but what's there to lose?"

Gleason decided to skip lunch and drove on to the station.

"In here, guys," Jay Halderman called out as they passed his office on the way to the detective's room.

"What's up, Lieutenant?" Gleason asked.

"We have a little problem. Sit down."

Gleason and Powers exchanged cautious glances as they took their seats.

"Homicide over at Porter Court in the Annex came in this morning," Halderman began. "I was stuck in a brass meeting. You all were in court. So guess who took the call?"

"No idea," Gleason said.

"Sonny Breaks."

"You can't be serious."

"Couldn't be more. Here's the deal. I've spoken with Breaks. He's now at the scene. Claims he has a suspect in custody. Both of you need to get over there ASAP!"

~ ~ ~

Jack was sitting handcuffed in the back seat of a patrol car parked in the circle on Porter Lane when the detectives' unmarked pulled up. Neither Gleason nor Powers noticed him as they hurried past.

"Where's Detective Breaks?" Gleason asked a cop at the gate.

"I believe he's inside the condo, sir."

He and Powers headed toward the yellow-taped building.

"Why so much of that stuff?" Powers asked. "Looks like Halloween on steroids. Wait, this is Monica Kuun's place. I was just here."

She picked up her pace.

Breaks was in the living room talking to a forensics tech. He turned to see who'd entered.

"Earl and Rachel," he greeted. "Glad you made it before we wrapped up."

"What've you got, Sonny?" Gleason asked.

"Vic's in the kitchen. Female. Appears to have been strangled. Doc's on the way. Also looks like the place was tossed. Probably looking for drugs or money to buy them."

Powers went over to the body.

"My God, that's Monica," she said, bending down.

Gleason stepped in for a closer look.

"I believe I saw this woman last night," he said, amazed. "Yeah, I recognize that dress. She was at Vinos and left with a guy."

"You know her?" Breaks asked.

"She was involved with something we're looking into," Powers told him.

"I have a suspect in custody," Breaks said, eyebrow quivering. "He admitted to being with her."

Gleason was surprised. Could it be the person he'd seen her with last night?

"Where is he?"

"In the patrol car," he motioned toward the street. "I'll have him transported as soon as I've finished here."

"I'd like to see him before that," Gleason said. "Rachel, wait here with Breaks. I'll be right back."

A doctor from the ME's office arrived to examine the body. Breaks pointed to the kitchen. Within minutes, Gleason was back.

"That's Jack Hunter you have out there," he told Breaks. "I know him. He's not the person I saw her with. I doubt Hunter had anything to do with this."

Breaks nervously cleared his throat.

"He acted suspicious when I questioned him," he said.

"Why were you questioning him?"

"He allegedly discovered the dead woman," Breaks said with a slight eyebrow tic. "Claims the door was open and he went in. Sounded fishy to me right from the start. Said he didn't know her at first. Then said he'd been helping her out since her boyfriend died. Maybe he was also checking out any valuables in the house. He could've been there when she walked in and caught him red-handed."

"So you think he's also a burglar?"

"There you go. Some guys will do anything for drug money. I asked point blank if he'd killed her. See if I could shock him into confessing. Sometimes they'll do that, you know."

Gleason knew better. But he did consider the possibility that Jack could somehow be involved. After all, this was Jack Hunter, trouble's best friend. Although he seriously doubted Jack had anything to do with murdering the woman or burglarizing her place.

"Okay, we'll go along with that for now," he said. "How did he react when you Mirandized him?"

Breaks hesitated before answering.

"I'll do that when I interview him at the station," he replied.

"Stop right there," Gleason said, holding up a hand. "You've interrogated him without reading him his rights first? And then placed him under arrest? That's the dumbest thing I've ever heard. Do you realize it could cost the whole case if it comes to court?"

"I didn't place him under arrest," Breaks said. "Just restrained him for everyone's protection."

"You interrogated him," Gleason counted off angrily. "You cuffed him. You placed him in custody."

"Sir, what about Judd Pittway?" Powers interrupted. "He's supposed to be leaving today."

Gleason shook his head in disbelief.

"Get on the phone to the hotels at the airport," he said quietly. "Maybe he hasn't left yet. Also, have someone call the airport to see if his plane is still there. I'm staying here until forensics come."

Gleason turned his attention back to Sonny Breaks.

"You return to the station and write up what you have. Don't show it to anyone. I want to see it first. And on your way out, have an officer bring Mr. Hunter to me. Without the handcuffs."

CHAPTER 13

JUDD PITTWAY HAD DEPARTED KEY WEST at 0700 hours according to the airport manager. Powers had gotten in touch with him first thing upon leaving the crime scene. His flight plan should put him at Lafayette Regional around mid-morning, the manager had said. Looking at her watch, Powers figured he was fat and happy in Louisiana by now.

She was in his room at the Double Tree. She'd gotten lucky on the first call to the hotels near the airport. Maid service had been held up at her request. But there'd been nothing of importance she could find. Just a rumpled bed and a couple of wet towels on the bathroom floor.

However, she had called for a forensic team. There could be useable DNA on the bed sheets and in the bathroom sink. If it belonged to Judd Pittway and matched any found on Monica Kuun that would be incriminating. She remembered the water bottle he'd drunk from in the interview room. Christ, if only they'd saved that! Well, how were they have to known then?

She'd also have the place dusted for prints. The room was probably alive with them from past guests but Pittway's were bound to be there, too. Should they also be in the condo, this would be a different game.

The forensic team had finished its job and left. She decided to wrap it up herself and return to the police station. She phoned Gleason and filled him in before leaving the hotel. He was at the desk when she walked into the detectives' room.

"You want a coffee, sir?"

Gleason nodded and she made two cups.

"How'd it go with Mr. Hunter?" she asked, returning and settling into her chair.

"Sonny Breaks had no business being there," Gleason grumbled. "Not only did he screw up by talking with Hunter, he's put us behind in the investigation. I'm going to see to it that he's knocked back to patrol."

Powers grinned and took a sip of coffee.

"Are we being sued?" she asked.

"We should be. And we would be if it'd been anyone else."

"I have to tell you I was surprised when Detective Breaks said he considered him as a suspect," Powers said. "Then having not Mirandized him, tsk, tsk."

"Yeah, Hunter is a lot of things, mostly a pain in the butt, but he's no killer. Anyway, he had an alibi. Up with some lady all night."

Powers felt a slight pang upon hearing that. All night with some lady? She couldn't explain why that would've bothered her.

"Oh?" she said.

"Old friend of his," Gleason continued. "Recently back in town. I called her to verify Hunter's story."

"Wonder who owns the condo in Porter Court?" Powers asked, changing the subject.

"What difference does that make?"

"None, I guess. Just that now two people have died there. If I owned it, I'd be bugged by that. Probably want to sell the thing."

"Could be some corporation owns it," Gleason said. "Wouldn't bother them at all. Just a rental. Anyway, it'll be awhile before we release it and they can put it on the market."

"Umm, probably right," Powers mused. "What about the person you saw with the Kuun women?"

"I'll talk with the bartender. He might know him."

"There's also Judd Pittway to consider, sir. This whole business with Monica Kuun is one contradiction after another. I don't care how much animosity there was between her and the brothers, she, not the lawyer, should've called them to say their dad had died. And here's another thing. Monica claimed they had no problem with her marrying Dewitt Pittway. Laid out the welcome mat. Going to be one big happy family. Yet Judd couldn't stand her."

"Didn't he say that the woman was from New Orleans?"

"Something about an escort service, I believe. Though she told me she was a fashion model."

"We should run her prints through the system," Gleason said. "If she was a working girl, she might have a record."

"Good idea, sir. Judd also told us that he had no intention of seeing Monica but that doesn't mean he didn't. I had forensics comb his hotel room. Hopefully, they can pick up his DNA and get a match on her body. Also, his prints might be at the crime scene."

"Well, that would certainly put the icing on the cake. Things are pretty busy with the lab, though. Could take a while. Be nice to talk with Pittway again."

"Shall I book us a flight to New Orleans, sir?"

~ ~ ~

Jack sat alone on a bench in the tiny park next to the Key West library. A chicken pecking at something interesting on the ground beneath some shrubbery across from him, the surrounding trees aflutter with twittering birds. It was early afternoon and traffic was light on the passing street.

Gleason had checked out his story and appeared to have been satisfied. Rather than stick around any longer, he'd decided to take a walk and had ended up here. The park offered a calm that he needed at the moment.

Key West had left him bruised lately and it was time to get the island back on *his* terms. But before giving that any more thought, he phoned Ruby Steele.

"Someone was murdered?" she asked.

"The woman staying across from me," Jack said.

"The detective didn't tell me he was calling about a murder."

"Guess he didn't want to tip his hand," he said, then added with a little laugh, "So you wouldn't try to cover for me."

Ruby had left Key West in fear for her life over something Jack had done. Now she was starting to have that same old feeling.

"And you're involved in this?" she asked.

"No."

"Then I don't understand why the police needed to know where you were last night."

"I found the body."

Ruby took in a breath.

"You see, this other cop thought I did it," Jack explained. "He was a jerk. But everything's okay now."

A long pause.

"Jack, I have to run. Got a ton of things to do."

"See you later?"

She was already gone.

~ ~ ~

I Shot the Sheriff was into the second stanza by the time Gleason had wrestled the phone from his pocket.

"This is Gleason," he answered in a rush.

"My, my, detective," Alice admonished playfully, "didn't your momma teach you any manners?"

She'd caught him in the police station parking lot.

"I'm just leaving work," he said. "Let me get in my car."

"Take your time, honey, I'm on the clock."

Biting his lip he slid into the front seat and shut the door. The interior was stifling. He started the engine and turned on the air conditioning.

"Okay, what's up?"

"Had a talk with your best friend, Detective Lundy. Lovely man. Seems the police were at Frank's shop on a vehicle theft warrant. Your little brother-in-law was allegedly running a chop shop. While there, they discovered a shitload of meth in his desk. Possible unlawful search since you wouldn't expect to find a stolen Harley hidden in a desk drawer. Lawyer should check that angle. Other thing is, Lundy says they have a witness who claims Frank sold him drugs."

"What about the stolen motorcycles?" Gleason asked. "Anything to it?"

"No evidence. But if you're into conspiracy theories, the meth might've been planted like your little sister claims."

"So you've found nothing we didn't already know," Gleason said sourly.

"Chin up, darling, Alice is on the case."

Gleason pulled out of the parking lot and headed to Vinos. He wanted to question the bartender, who should be coming on shift about now. Unable to find a parking space on Duval, he drove home and walked back.

Happy Hour was underway and it was standing room only at the bar. Gleason made his way to the end and sidled into a space. The bartender recognized him and poured a glass of merlot.

"Thanks," Gleason said. "Remember that guy who was here last night with the good-looking lady? Sat a couple of seats over. Had on a great dress."

"Hang on a sec while I take care of those folks down at the other end."

Gleason took a sip of wine and checked out the room. A few minutes later the bartender got back to him.

"Okay, what was it again you wanted to know?" he asked.

"Guy with a terrific-looking woman sitting right here last night," Gleason said, pointing. "You know him?"

"Oh, yeah," the bartender nodded. "Some looker. That was O-B with her."

"You know how I can get in touch with him? It's kind of important."

"He tends bar at that new place ... what the hell's its name?" He thought for a moment. "Comix. Think it's a gay bar. You ready for another merlot?"

~ ~ ~

Detective Powers had just gotten off the phone with the medical examiner's office. The autopsy had been completed. Charles Gibbs could be released to the mortuary. She picked up her phone again and called the boy's father.

He answered on the third ring and she explained the nature of her call and that it would probably be best if he made arrangements with someone there to bring Charley home. Gibbs thanked her and said he would do that and also that he thought he might fly down to Key West and ride with his son back to New Bern.

Powers wished him well.

~ ~ ~

Gleason recognized the man behind the bar as soon as he walked in. He found a vacant stool, sat and looked around. The bar was horseshoe-shaped, one end against a mirrored wall with liquor bottles stacked on glass shelves in front. Framed comic book artwork decorated the other walls, which were painted vibrant blue. Lighting was low and campy elevator music played softly from somewhere.

Normally, in a situation like this, he'd identify himself and ask if there was somewhere – perhaps a small room – where they could talk in private. Depending on how that went, any further conversation would take place in an interview room at the police station.

The bartender came over to him.

"What can I get you, my man?"

"You're O-B, right?'" Gleason asked.

"Yeah," he grinned, cocking his head. "You look familiar. Have we met?"

"I'm Detective Earl Gleason with KWPD. Somewhere we can talk?"

Caution flashed momentarily in the bartender's eyes.

"Now?" he asked.

"It would be appreciated."

"I'll have to get someone to fill in."

Five minute later, they were in a cramped office on the second floor.

"I'm curious," Gleason smiled. "What does O-B stand for?"

"Nickname. I'm Oscar Boyd."

"Guy I grew up with had the same nickname," Gleason said.

"I really need to get back downstairs. So if we could get on with whatever you want to know?"

"Sure, you originally from Key West?" Gleason asked.

"From Miami. Been here for a couple of years. What's this about?"

"I'm interested in the woman you were sitting with at Vinos last night. Is she a friend?"

Boyd scrunched his face in thought.

"Oh, that was Monica," he laughed. "No, she's not a friend."

"Really? You two seemed to have a lot to talk about."

"She just happened to be sitting at the bar when I came in. I'd never seen her before."

"You must be psychic," Gleason chuckled. "Never saw her before yet you know her name."

"She introduced herself. In my business, you remember names."

"Okay, I'll buy that. Where did you and Monica go afterwards?"

"I went to Aqua. I have no idea where she went."

"You left Vinos together."

"So, that's the big deal?" Boyd laughed. "She split the next block. She got a phone call. Said goodbye to me and that was it."

Gleason considered whether he should ask him to come to the station. He decided to hold off for the moment.

"How long did you stay at Aqua?"

"Couple of hours," Boyd shrugged.

He could've gone from there to the Annex, Gleason thought. Monica could have given him her address.

"Is there anyone who can verify that?" he asked.

"Yeah, my husband. He bartends there. We went home after he'd closed out. What's this about anyway?"

"The woman is dead."

~ ~ ~

Feeling somewhat disappointed, Gleason walked back to his apartment. He had ascertained Boyd's alibi with a call to his partner at Aqua. That didn't quite take him off the hook, however. The two of them could have gone to Truman Annex afterwards. He knew at best that was a long, long shot and very, very unlikely, but he wasn't ready to dismiss anything at this point. He'd get a DNA swab from Boyd and his hubby later. He'd also pull their prints from DMV.

He came to where he'd parked the car by his building. He should drive to the station and write up everything he'd learned while it was still fresh in his mind. Instead, he went on upstairs.

A string of meows cried from behind the door while he fumbled for the key, demanding that he go straight to the kitchen. After feeding and watering Mitts, he put on a CD – Variations on a Theme by Rossini – and opened the cabinet for a bottle of merlot to take out on the balcony. Empty. How could that be? He knew he'd bought a case just the other day. Nothing else to do but run to the liquor store.

CHAPTER 14

DR. BLAKE HARDY HAD DECIDED on his own to proceed with the autopsy on Dewitt Pittway and not wait for any word from the lawyer. He called Gleason to tell him that it was scheduled for that morning since the detective had asked to be present.

"Detective Gleason hasn't come in yet, doctor," Rachel Powers said. "I expect him any minute."

"We'll get the show going at ten," Blake told her. "You're invited, too."

Powers thanked the doctor and hung up. She looked at her watch. It was a little after nine. Should she call him?

To her relief, Gleason walked into the detective's room carrying a cup of coffee.

"Good morning, sir," she piped.

"Damn alarm didn't go off," he said. "Anything new?"

Actually, the alarm clock *did* ring. Gleason hadn't heard it because he was outside on the balcony, where he'd fallen asleep the night before. Mitts had awakened him by pouncing on his chest and purring.

"They're autopsying Pittway at ten," Powers said. "We should leave soon."

Gleason felt like begging off. He didn't know if he was up to witnessing the disassembling of another human. He'd seen enough violence lately. At the moment, stepping into an autopsy suite would be like visiting a crime scene. Also, his stomach was a little queasy this morning.

He'd read somewhere that the retirement age for many homicide detectives was fifty-three. While he was nowhere near that, the idea of calling it quits had a certain appeal. But then what?

"Let's go," he said. "I'll drive."

~ ~ ~

Jack had finished vacuuming the upstairs bedrooms and now was busy with dry mopping the living room and kitchen. Earlier, he'd taken care of the bathrooms. He began with them in his cleaning routine. No reason in particular other than that you could see the immediate results of a well-scrubbed bath, which was gratifying. He wasn't compulsive about cleaning. It was an every-couple-of-weeks-or-so event. He just wasn't a messy person. He ought to hire a maid, he'd told himself a thousand times. The rental agency offered maid service. But the idea of having one was just something he could never get his head around. There *had been* a maid when he and Pamela were married. She'd had the woman long before they had even met and couldn't live without her. He had always felt a little self-conscious about having someone come in. Not only that, but in truth, he kind of enjoyed doing the job himself.

The place finally clean, he grabbed the trash bag and took it to the dumpster. Nearing the steel container, he went for a three-pointer but the bag bounced off the closed top and plopped on the ground behind. The groundskeepers would shut the dumpster when it was full. He went around to pick it up and saw another bag lying there. He chuckled, thinking it was probably a missed shot by another would-be basketball player. He reached down for it as well as his own and something familiar inside fell out. Something he now remembered seeing before.

~ ~ ~

"Mr. Pittway died from heart failure," Blake Hardy stated, walking over to where Gleason and Powers stood. Gleason had just returned to the autopsy suite after taking one of several breaks outside. Powers, however, had stoically remained inside the entire time. Behind him, Dewitt Pittway's nude body lay on a stainless steel examination table. The coarsely stitched Y-incision ran chest to groin.

"And here's what killed him."

The doctor held a small metal device about the size of a fifty-cent piece and a little thicker.

"This is a pacemaker," he explained. "Think about it as a tiny computer that keeps your heart on the straight and narrow. From beating too fast or slow."

Gleason recalled a case where the victim had been so frightened by a snake that'd been put in his bed that his heart had called it quits. Would a pacemaker have helped?

"The most common reasons for needing one are bradycardia and heart block," Hardy said. "Bradycardia is a slower than normal heartbeat. Heart block is when something's screwed up in the heart's electrical system."

"Like a blown fuse?" Gleason wise-guyed. He loved joshing the medical examiner, all good-naturedly.

Hardy smiled and continued.

"Pacemakers are programmable, which means their rates can be changed. The cardiologist can do this. I'd like to see Mr. Pittway's medical records. That would tell us what's been going on with him. Maybe he has a history of heart disease. Or it runs in the family. Find out what drugs he takes."

"So what happened with the pacemaker?" Gleason asked.

"That *is* the question, detective," Hardy said.

"Wouldn't Pittway have known something was wrong?"

"Not necessarily. If his heart rate changed, he could've experienced a shortness of breath, possibly dizziness. Could even faint. But he would have to be awake to realize what was happening. I understand he was discovered unconscious in bed. If the attack occurred while he was sleeping, he might not have felt anything."

"Aren't cellphones dangerous around pacemakers?" Powers asked. "Maybe he'd been using one."

"It used to be that people wearing one were told to stay away from them but not anymore," Hardy said. "They aren't powerful enough. Even the old phones weren't really. Same with microwaves and the like. All of those things are much better shielded now so it's no problem. But I wouldn't recommend you have a MRI scan. The danger there is the prolonged exposure to the magnetic field."

"In other words, don't lean against the refrigerator door if it has magnets on it," Gleason joked to Powers. He was beginning to feel a little uptight. The humor helped.

"Actually, there's something to that," Hardy said. "It's called the six-inch rule."

"You're kidding," Gleason said.

"Not at all. A magnet has to have a field strength of at least ten gauss to deactivate a pacemaker. For example, the magnet in a stereo speaker runs about one hundred gauss right next to it but six inches away? Zero. So the lesson is if you're wearing a pacemaker, keep your distance. Don't hug the speakers on your hi-fi."

"Back to the pacemaker," Powers said. "Can it be tested to find out why it quit working?"

"Yes, the lab will tell us. There's one more thing. I feel Pittway may have been in the early onset of Alzheimer's. I'm going to have that tested."

~ ~ ~

Now in the car, Powers turned to Gleason while he drove them back to the police station.

"Pretty gruesome way to spend a morning," she said.

"That's one way of describing it," Gleason answered.

"Wonder if Pittway really didn't want an autopsy? I mean, suppose Monica was telling the truth? I kind of felt sorry for him."

Gleason shot her a look.

"There he was, taken apart and then just tossed back together. I know that's how it works but still, after seeing a few autopsies, I might not want one either."

Gleason laughed, feeling better now.

"I knew a guy who was buried at sea," he said. "How do you feel about that?"

"Ugh, I couldn't stand it! All those creepy things on the bottom crawling over me."

"Yeah, I feel the same way about being buried," Gleason agreed. "Worms wiggling their way in. Free to go anywhere they damn please."

"There's always cremation," Powers suggested.

"Not bad," Gleason nodded. "At least, it's done and over with."

"I'd want my ashes thrown to the wind," Powers said wistfully. "Then I could magically float above the world."

"How about scattered on the ocean?" Gleason offered. "I've always wanted to take a cruise."

"Off Key West?"

"No, I'm thinking more of the South Pacific. Hawaii's pretty or that island the French artist liked to paint. Know him?"

"You mean Paul Gauguin? That was in Tahiti."

The two cops bantered back and forth all the way to the station. Leaving both in a much better mood when they arrived.

"I think we should look more into Dewitt Pittway and Monica Kuun," Gleason said. "Check out that town where he lived. Put in a call to the local police department there. Don't know what we can expect to find out but maybe it'll just get the ball rolling."

"I'll get right on it, sir."

Powers quickly discovered that Louisiana had more different law enforcement agencies than even Florida. State police, levee police, campus police, parish sheriffs, it went on and on. Reading through her reports, she reaffirmed that Pittway lived in Cleopus in St. Julian Parish. Not finding a listing for a municipal department, she tried the sheriff's office.

"St. Julian Sheriff's Station. This is Ann Creely."

CHAPTER 15

THE FIRE DEPARTMENT HAD QUICKLY extinguished the blaze but the kitchen was ruined. Water everywhere. Billy surveyed the damage.

He wouldn't be cooking on that stove anytime soon. Refrigerator and freezer looked pretty good. He got a mop from the closet to begin cleaning up but only stood with it in the middle of the floor.

Fortunately, the restaurant had been empty of customers when the fire had started. Breakfast was over and they were setting up for lunch. Billy was helping in the dining area. Someone smelled smoke. Billy threw open the kitchen door and was greeted by a blast of heat. The stove was ablaze and flames were threatening to spread.

Fire Engine No. 7111 arrived within minutes of the call. In no time, the fire was put out. And to everyone's relief, it hadn't burned farther than around the stove.

Billy had thanked the firemen and said he wished he could make them sandwiches to take back. He'd then sent the help home, stuck a closed sign on the door and called Jack.

~ ~ ~

"Billy, you in there?" Jack shouted, banging on the glass window and pressing his face against it to see inside. "Come unlock the door."

"Missed all the excitement, hee-hee," Billy said, letting in Jack. "I'd been thinking about replacing that damn stove."

"Is everyone all right?" Jack asked.

"A little grease fire is all. Everybody else has cleared out, Jack. Gone home. No need to stick around here. We're closed."

Jack followed Billy into the kitchen.

"Pretty bad fire," he said, taking in the ruined stove and blackened wall. "Lucky it wasn't worse."

"Just starting to mop up this water," Billy said, then felt a little lightheaded. "Think I better sit down for a moment."

"Don't worry about the water, Billy. Go sit out there. I'll take care of the kitchen."

Jack led Billy back to the dining room and seated him in a chair. He was concerned for his friend. Something wasn't right.

"You going to be okay?" he asked.

"Think I ought to call Sparrow and let him know what's happened? He might be upset when he finds out about that ol' stove."

"I'll do of that, too. You take it easy, all right?"

Jack phoned Sparrow Lovewell, who was also a partner in the restaurant. After he explained about the fire and his concern for Billy, Sparrow agreed to come there and take Billy home. Once that'd been settled, he went for another look at the damage.

No question, they'd have to put in a new kitchen. Too bad Melody, the woman contractor he'd used a couple of times before, had moved away. She did good work. He'd have to make some calls.

"Sparrow's on his way," Jack told Billy, returning to the dining room. "When was the last time you had a physical?"

"You talking about seeing a doctor? Hell, Jack, I ain't been sick. Why'd I want to see the doctor?"

"Right, well, I'm going to make an appointment for you."

Billy started to put up a fuss but Jack cut him off.

"Company rule," he said. "All partners must get an annual physical. It's in the contract."

The only contract they'd ever had was a handshake.

"Don't argue," Jack said before Billy could make that point. "I just added it."

Sparrow arrived and, after having a quick look around and a short conversation with Jack, left the restaurant with an exhausted Billy.

Jack finished mopping up. He'd also found a floor fan in a storage room and put it to work drying out the place. Now, he sat at a table in the dining room to begin making those phone calls, the first being to Derrick Bean at Stella by Starlight about closing the Inedible Cafe. But before he could punch in the number, a man walked in through the open front door.

"Kitchen's closed," Jack said dismissively, his attention on the phone.

"Bar open?" the man asked.

Jack looked at him and grinned.

"That's a terrific idea," he told him.

~ ~ ~

"This is Sheriff JT Wainscot ... uh, what was the name again, detective?"

"Powers, sir. Rachel Powers. I'm with the Key West Police Department."

The sheriff had been leaving the office when Powers called. After she'd explained why she was calling, Ann Creely had rushed out to the parking lot and stopped him before he'd gotten away.

"Detective Powers, it's a pleasure to be of service, ma'am. What can we do for you?"

Powers thought the man had a nice voice but she could barely understand a word he was saying.

"We are currently investigating a suspicious death which may be connected to a homicide, Sheriff Wainscot. Both victims are from your area."

"Well, ma'am, St. Julian Parish covers a lot of ground. You have names for these unfortunate folks?"

"Monica Kuun and Dewitt Pittman. They're from Cleopus."

"Dewitt Pittman is well-known around here," JT said. "Can't say I'm familiar with the other person. Which one was the homicide?"

Powers ear was beginning to get in step with the cadence of the Cajun-flavored accent.

"Monica Kuun. We haven't received an autopsy report on her yet, but it appeared to have been a strangulation. We do have the medical examiner's report on Mr. Pittway. He died of an apparent heart attack. However, there are some questions, which is why the medical examiners' office is involved. The man wore a pacemaker."

"Well, that's interesting, detective, but how are the two deaths related?"

"Monica Kuun and Dewitt Pittman were supposedly engaged to be married."

"That so?" Wainscot said. "Dewitt getting married again? I forget what number that would be. No disrespect intended."

"Respectfully, she would've been number three, sir. She and Mr. Pittway were in Key West on vacation. He had a heart attack the night they arrived. Miss Kuun was murdered shortly afterwards."

"And you believe one death had something to do with the other?" JT asked. "Do you have any evidence to suggest that?"

"Right now all we have is coincidence, sir. We spoke with one of his sons, Judd Pittway. He came here after being notified of his father's death. He wasn't thrilled about the upcoming nuptials. Even accused Miss Kuun of having an agenda of sorts. As in gold digging."

"Do you suspect he's involved in the woman's death?" Wainscot asked seriously.

"He could be a person of interest, sir. It'd help to talk further with him."

"He's no longer in Key West, I take it."

"No, sir. Flew home this morning. "

"Well, back to my original question. What can we do for you?"

"I'd like to come there and have that talk with Judd Pittway, with your approval, of course. Appears to be a very unusual family."

"Be happy to cooperate," he said. "I'll need some proof that you're who you say you are. One other thing about the Pittways, they may be unusual but they're also an old family in St. Julian Parrish. Careful where you step."

"Thank you, sir. Oh, and Sheriff Wainscot, I'd appreciate it if you kept Monica Kuun's death under your hat for the time being."

"No problem, ma'am, I might pass on my condolences to the family about Dewitt, however."

That out of the way, Powers next needed to see Halderman. She realized she'd put the cart before the pony by talking with the sheriff first. What if she couldn't get approval from her own department for a trip to Louisiana?

"Got a minute, sir?" she asked, knocking on the lieutenant's door.

"Sure, Powers, come in."

Ten minutes later she was out of his office and without approval. Tight money, Halderman had explained. She'd known he was a budget wonk but she hadn't expected this. Then, to make matters worse, he had said the brass would consider it a boondoggle. "New Orleans!" he'd snorted. And then had added perhaps she would like tickets to a Saints game. Her attempt at levity by reminding him that it wasn't football season had only earned her a dismissive wave of the hand.

Gleason was at the homicide desk in the detective's room

"Think I just screwed up, sir," she said, pulling back her chair.

"Remember Oscar Boyd?" Gleason said, looking up from his computer. "Guy I saw with Monica Kuun the night she was murdered. Seems he was once arrested for aggravated assault in Miami. Bad boy."

"I thought he had an alibi," Powers said. "Home with his beloved all night."

"Alibis are just excuses. Some are better than others. Should've checked him out earlier. I'm going to get a DNA swab from Boyd now. Something else, too. He said Monica left him after getting a telephone call. I don't remember seeing a cellphone at the scene, do you?"

"Not really. I looked through her purse. If there'd been one, it would have gone to forensics. No billfold, either. I know she had one. Her bag's in the evidence room. I'll check it out again."

"Let's do that right away," Gleason said. "So what's the problem?"

CHAPTER 16

A PAIR OF SLEEK WAHOOS RESTED in an ice chest on the kitchen floor. The fish had been caught that morning. Derrick Bean pulled one out and placed it on a metal-covered table top.

"You going to want a piece of this fish tonight, Jack?"

"Save it for the paying customers. I'll be busy at the restaurant."

Derrick made a quick cut behind the fish's head with a filleting knife.

"So you think that will work?" he asked in his clipped British accent.

Jack had explained his idea about keeping the Undrinkable Bar open while the kitchen was being redone. Derrick was skeptical.

"People expect something to eat at a restaurant," he said.

"So I'll serve bar food," Jack told him.

Derrick smiled.

"Get a barrel of roasted peanuts like the Chart Room has," Jack continued. "Maybe I'll get some boiled eggs, too."

"Sounds yummy."

"Look, it's just an idea," Jack said defensively. "I hate to see the place closed for a month or however long it takes."

Derrick sliced off a long fillet.

"It's the Inedible Cafe, Jack."

"And?"

"And it has a reputation. You don't want to sully that with peanuts and boiled eggs."

"So what do you suggest?"

"Let me look at the menu."

Derrick studied it and frowned.

He then divided the fillet into several thick pieces.

~ ~ ~

"Ever been to Flamingo, Lieutenant?"

Gleason was in Jay Halderman's office. He'd gone there on Power's behalf. Halderman replied to the question with a cautious look.

"Pimple on the ass of the Everglades," Gleason said. "Used to be a fishing village 'way back when. After the fish left, it became a ghost town. Hurricane Wilma wiped out what was left standing. Only thing there now are mosquitos the size of hawks. Once took my ex-wife to see it."

"You're thinking of taking her again?" Halderman smiled. "That ought to win her back."

Gleason returned the smile with a deadpan look.

"No, but it's a good description of where Powers wants to go."

"Oh, c'mon, Earl," Halderman laughed. "Powers wants to go on a boondoggle to New Orleans."

"Cleopus is not New Orleans," Gleason said. "It's a crossroad at best. I looked it up. Middle of nowhere out in the swamps."

"So what does she expect to find there? Besides alligators and water moccasins."

"It's the Pittway family home. She needs to ask around. Be on the scene. Find out more about them. There's a connection between the two deaths."

"I don't know, Earl. The captain will have a fit. Could she drive there?"

Gleason laughed.

"It's four hours just from here to Miami, Jay. Take two days to drive to Louisiana."

"New Orleans is going to be a problem," Halderman said, shaking his head.

Gleason smiled inwardly at the irony lobbying for Powers. He'd be pushing for himself to go there if it weren't for the problem in Bradenton. He couldn't risk being out of town right now.

"This whole business with Pittway is screwy, Jay. Big fuss over the autopsy. One of Pittway's kids hits town pissed off to hell. Bad blood between the family and Monica Kuun. She turns up dead the next morning. Kid splits for Louisiana. There's something else, too. This guy Oscar Boyd who was with her the night she died. Said she got a telephone call before leaving him. We didn't find any phone at the condo. Could've been taken. Along with her billfold. This whole thing could've been a robbery gone wrong. Powers is going through the crime scene evidence again."

"That's being productive," Halderman nodded. "She should spend her time here rather than waste it in Louisiana."

Gleason brushed that off, and proceeded to lay out good reasons for a bayou visit.

"Judd Pittway is still on our list and he's back there. And he did mention that Monica Kuun was from New Orleans. Hinted about her working for an escort service. Could be a party girl. If that's true, she might have an arrest record. We've put her prints in the system. May be someone else in New Orleans who knows her. Meanwhile, I'm continuing to follow up on Oscar Boyd."

He paused before setting the hook.

"But I believe this case will eventually be solved in Louisiana."

"All right, detective," Halderman said, showing his palms in surrender. "You've made your point. I'll see what I can do. But believe me, the captain's going be looking at this with a magnifying glass. Powers will have to account for every dime."

Gleason gave a wolfish grin.

"The sheriff there sounds helpful," he said. "Maybe he'll put her up in the barn. That'll save money."

~ ~ ~

Sheriff JT Wainscot pulled out of the station's parking lot in his triple black '68 Corvette. The car was a survivor. Original as the day it'd rolled off the production line. JT had once considered having it painted and the upholstery redone but a friend who understood the value of the car brought him to his senses. The 435 hp engine had eaten the twenty miles to Cleopus before it'd even completely warmed up.

JT spotted Judd Pittway sitting in a chair on the front porch that ran across the front of his house. It wasn't because he and Judd were friends that he'd recognized him – everyone in St. Julian Parish knew the Pittways. He drove into the driveway and stopped.

"What can I do for you today, Sheriff?" Judd called from the porch. "Seems you're dressed for business."

JT had on his uniform.

"Just came by to pay my respects," he said, going up the steps. "Sorry about your dad."

"Get you something to drink? "Judd asked, getting to his feet and shaking JT's hand. "I'm having iced tea."

"No, thanks. Dewitt's passing came as a surprise. Didn't realize he'd been sick."

"Huh, probably surprised him, too," Judd chuckled. "Truth is, he hadn't been sick at all. That flu going around last year 'bout the only thing. But I guess you never know."

"Only the good Lord knows," JT agreed. "Understand he was about to get married."

"Don't believe that'd been announced to the papers," Judd said. "Who'd you hear that from?"

"Hell, son, this is St. Julians Parish," JT laughed. "Word travels on the breeze."

Judd grinned.

"Doesn't matter now," he said. "His betrothed can go the hell back to New Orleans. Bye, bye, Monica. Don't let the door hit you in the butt on your way out."

He made a waving gesture.

"That her name?" JT asked. "Monica?"

"Monica Kuun. Great body, good lay. Those were the ground rules for dad's dalliances. But marriage? He'd never have gone through with that unless he'd totally lost his marbles is all I can say."

"Gather you and the lucky lady didn't get along."

"If you want to put it mildly, you could say that."

"Any particular reason?"

Judd frowned.

"Any particular reason for your asking, Sheriff?"

JT laughed and stood to leave.

"None at all, Judd. Just the lawman in me getting too nosy. Bad habit I can't seem to shake. When's the funeral?"

"Soon as dad gets back from Key West."

The Corvette loped along at a much slower pace back to the sheriff's station in Bonnet. He hadn't mentioned Monica Kuun's murder, as the Key West detective had requested. His impression, however, was that Judd Pittway had nothing to do with it. The man obviously didn't care for the woman and was dead-set against the marriage. But enough to kill the would-be bride? At the moment, it was only a curious question. He'd phone Detective Powers later. Right now he was enjoying a ride through the bayou with the top down.

CHAPTER 17

POWERS SAW THE FEDEX PACKAGE waiting at the front door as if wanting to be let in. She was excited that it'd finally arrived and grabbed it up even before sticking the house key in the lock. Inside, she went straight to the bedroom and placed the box on the bed. She dug her fingers under the flaps to rip it open. But the tape wouldn't tear. Back to the kitchen for a knife, she returned and quickly sliced through the binding and removed what she hoped would be a medical breakthrough.

However, the magnetic mattress pad looked more like something you'd find in a baby's crib. It was an inch thick and quilted.

A pamphlet was included. She thumbed through it. It explained how strategically- placed magnets – each rated at nearly four-thousand gauss – gave curved lines of magnetic flux to soothe aches and pains and reduce inflammation. Furthermore, the pad itself was designed to keep them as close to the body as possible. There were happy customer reviews, too. People swore by the thing.

She threw back the bed covers. Pulled off the bottom sheet and smoothed the pad onto the mattress. Then she stretched out.

Fifteen minutes later she got up and – amazingly – her back felt better. Swear to God.

~ ~ ~

"Billy said he was using your company now. I was wondering if you could drop off a couple cases of chardonnay at the Inedible Cafe? Expecting a busy night."

Jack was on the phone with Janine Brown. She owned a new wine delivery service named Latitude 24.

"Billy favors Riche Vineyard in Sonoma," Jack said. "That's in California. Come to think of it, we might need a couple cases of red. He likes Cakebread Cabernet Sauvignon. They're in Napa. Next town over from Sonoma. How's business?"

"Well, we're on the map."

"Come in through the front," Jack told her, missing the joke. "The kitchen burned down and the backdoor is locked."

"But you need the wine for tonight, right?"

"Yeah, the bar's open."

"Of course it is."

~ ~ ~

Alice, eastbound on Alligator Alley, needed to make a decision. Key West was six more hours of steady driving at best. Fort Lauderdale was less than an hour ahead. A comfortable room at a motel, nice meal somewhere good, and an early start in the morning won the toss.

Forty-five minutes later she'd checked in, gotten a solid recommendation on a restaurant and was now calling Gleason.

"Hello, darling, this is the world's greatest private detective with wonderful news. Your racist brother-in-law is off the hook. Now he can go back to burning crosses."

Gleason had just walked in when the phone rang.

"What was that? The cat's going crazy. I couldn't hear."

Mitts was entwined around Gleason's legs beseeching him with loud meows for dinner.

"I said the case is closed," she repeated. "They decided not to prosecute."

Gleason went out onto the deck.

"That's amazing, Alice. What happened?"

"It's a short story that I'll tell you tomorrow when I'm back in town. Right now I'm off on a hot date with a restaurant. Bye."

Gleason stood holding his cellphone, a big grin on his face. He sat down in a chair. Mitts jumped into his lap.

Dropped the case, he said aloud. And smiled again.

Could've been for a lot of reasons. Maybe even that the guy was innocent. Charlotte must be relieved. He certainly was himself. She'd probably be calling to thank him. He'd get the lowdown from her.

He got up. Mitts ran to the kitchen. Gleason followed and poured himself a glass of wine. He fed the cat and decided that Alice had the right idea. He'd also go out to a restaurant tonight.

~ ~ ~

"Fish sandwiches," Jack said, choking a laugh.

"Trust me, Jack," Derrick smiled. "A mate of mine in Bermuda invented them. Gave me his recipe. Uses raisin bread. Already have the fish ready."

The two of them were at Stella by Starlight. The restaurant was about to open.

"Sounds disgusting," Jack said, making a face. "Besides they'll be cold by the time they get to the Inedible, Derrick. Nobody wants a cold fish sandwich no matter what kind of bread it's on. Well, I guess so if it's tuna salad. That what you're talking about?"

"Nope. Hot off the stove. Here's what we'll do. You tell the people that there's a special tonight. In fact, it's so special nothing else is being served. Call me on my phone as soon as you get an order. Not Stella's – mine. I'll cook it right then and Jennifer will delivery it immediately to the restaurant. She'll need your motor scooter, by the way."

Jack shook his head.

"Peanuts would be a lot easier," he said. "What if you get busy here?"

"Not to worry, Jack. I've got a system."

~ ~ ~

Twilight had settled in on Michael's patio when Gleason walked through the restaurant's gate. He'd parked on Southard around the corner from Margaret Street. The bar had a few vacant seats and he took one. Suzette was bartending.

"Hi, what can I get you?" she asked.

"Glass of merlot."

She put a menu in front of him.

"In case you're hungry."

Gleason turned to take in the patio. Couples chatted quietly at tables. Men casually dressed. Women alluringly attired.

He sipped his wine and picked up the menu.

~ ~ ~

"It's crazy here," Jack shouted into the phone. "What'd you put in those sandwiches?"

"Didn't I tell you they'd be fantastic?" Derrick laughed. "How many do you need this time? I'm running short on fish."

"Give me what you have and I'll tell everyone we're sold out after that."

Derrick said he was on it and Jennifer would be there in fifteen minutes. Jack got busy again backing up the bar. He'd just refilled the cooler with ice when his phone rang again. It was Derrick on the line.

"You won't believe this, Jack. Someone just made off with your scooter."

"How can that be?"

"Parked out front. Jenifer left the key in the ignition."

"What about the fish sandwiches?"

"I'll call a taxi."

~ ~ ~

Gleason finished the last of his wine and asked for the check. It'd been a great evening. Good idea to have gone out.

Suzette handed him the folder and he looked over the bill. Seemed in order, although the wine portion was higher than he'd have thought. A closer look revealed four glasses of merlot. He paid and left for his car.

The street was completely dark and he needed to watch where he stepped on the uneven sidewalk. In fact, he almost stumbled.

Slipping behind the wheel, he gave himself a little sobriety test before starting the engine. Tapping his thumb with each finger on both hands, he only missed once. He drove off.

He was approaching Elizabeth Street when his rearview mirror turned red. A siren whooped twice behind him. He pulled over, stopped, rolled down his window and placed both hands on the steering wheel.

The patrol car with its rack lights flashing sat behind him for a moment before the cop got out.

"Good evening, officer," Gleason said.

"Good evening, sir. May I see your driver's license?"

"My billfold's in my coat. Okay if I reach for it?"

"Do it slowly, sir."

Gleason was wearing a sports jacket. He removed the billfold, took out the licenses, and handed it to the cop.

"Thanks you, sir. I'll be right back."

The cop walked to his car and remained there for another couple of minutes before returning.

"There's a block on your car's plate," he said. "And also on your drivers' licenses."

"I'm with the department," Gleason told him, removing his police ID from his billfold.

The cop looked at it and nodded.

"Well, Detective Gleason, the reason I stopped you is that you were weaving. I can smell alcohol on your breath. How much have you had to drink tonight, sir?"

"I had dinner and, yeah, a glass of wine."

The cop nodded again.

"Where are you going now?" he asked.

"Home. I live just the other side of Duval."

"Well, sir, I think you're a little over the limit but here's what I'm going to do. You go ahead and drive there. I'll follow."

He returned Gleason's driver's license.

"Thank you, officer. I'll wait until you're back in your car before I leave."

Gleason took a deep breath. The cop switched off his rack lights and Gleason pulled away slowly, hands white-knuckling the steering wheel. He had the green light at Simonton, but a motor scooter sped through the intersection, running the red. Gleason hit his brakes.

His car suddenly filled with flashing red lights and Gleason's heart sank. The patrol car pulled around him, tires squealing, as he gunned it after the scooter.

Gleason made it home safely. The cat met him at the door.

CHAPTER 18

JACK HAD REPORTED THE THEFT that night and the next morning heard back from KWPD. His scooter had been found. They'd fished it out of the water about thirty feet from where Simonton Street ends and the Gulf of Mexico begins. A short docking pier at the tiny beach there had served as a launch pad.

The officer had said that the rider was in custody at the hospital jail ward. Jack could pick up the scooter at the police impound yard. However, he might want to bring a truck because he doubted seriously that it would run.

He was now at the Inedible Cafe waiting for a new stove and refrigerator to be delivered. He and Sparrow Lovewell had earlier moved the burned-out appliances to the alley. Jack had discovered that the fire hadn't done any structural damage but that the entire kitchen needed painting. Sparrow had mentioned that his sister had said something about his cousin painting houses. Jack had told him to send the guy over.

Sparrow had also updated him on Billy. He'd practically had to drag him to the doctor. They'd run a bunch of tests. And the doctor suspected Billy might've had a mild stroke but he wouldn't be sure until all the results were in.

Jack had insisted that Billy stay home and rest until they'd found out what was going on. Sparrow had promised he'd do his best but they both knew Billy.

~ ~ ~

"Detective Gleason took a personal day, Doctor Hardy," Powers said. "He'll be in tomorrow."

"Well, good for him. I wanted to let both of you know that I received Dewitt Pittway's medical records. Interesting reading."

Powers smiled broadly.

"I'm sure the detective wouldn't mind your telling me," she said.

"Mr. Pittway had a history of heart disease. It was being treated with medication. However, as his arrhythmia became more dangerous and he developed a severe form of bradycardia, the doctor recommended a pacemaker."

"So did that do the trick?" Powers asked. "Everything was hunky dory after he got the pacemaker?"

"Yep, as long as the pacemaker kept working as programmed. Otherwise, with someone in his condition, bad things can happen in a hurry."

"Would his doctor have done anything to change the programming?"

"There was no mention of it in the medical records."

"Maybe it was a malfunction in the pacemaker," Powers suggested. "Possible, right?"

"It tested out perfectly."

"I don't understand."

"The pacemaker reset itself the night he died. Threw everything out of whack. Something or someone had to have done that."

Powers felt a surge of excitement.

"Pittway's system had a high level of zoplidem tartrate in it," Hardy said. "That's a sleeping pill commonly known as Ambien. The normal dose would be around ten milligrams. His was around thirty."

"Would Pittway have overdosed himself?" Powers asked.

"It's a prescription drug. He'd have known the dosage. Curious, I didn't see any reference to it in his medical records. His doctor might not have listed it, though."

"What about the Alzheimer's? If he had dementia, could he have unknowingly overdosed?"

"I haven't received the test results on that yet but in my opinion, no."

"Then we're definitely talking about a homicide," Powers said.

"So far."

~ ~ ~

Gleason had holed up at home. He'd phoned Halderman first thing that morning saying he was coming down with something and it'd be better if he took the day off. The lieutenant had agreed and mentioned that there was a bug going around. The truth was Gleason had needed to think about where he was heading.

That patrol officer had gone out on a shaky limb by giving him that break. Had it been someone else who'd stopped him – the Sheriffs, for instance – he might be sitting in a cell now instead of on his nice deck. He didn't even know the man's name. Not that he had any intention of thanking him. Better to let the whole incident pass. He was sure the officer would prefer that, too.

But the fact remained – he'd had too much to drink.

And it wasn't just that he shouldn't have been driving. Of course he shouldn't have. The scarier part was it'd never occurred to him that he was that impaired. Yeah, yeah, the pitiful little sobriety test he'd given himself. He'd been too fucked up to even realize he'd flunked it. How long had this been going on?

How would he know? One day you're okay and then the day comes you're no longer okay. That's the treachery of alcohol.

So was he an alcoholic? He didn't believe he was. Alcoholism didn't run in his family. He wasn't one of those guys waking up in the gutter on Duval Street. But to be honest, he had been drinking a lot lately. Maybe he was just stressed out. Powers had noticed. Said he'd seemed distracted.

Even so, that didn't excuse what had happened. He'd been stopped for DUI. He'd had too much to drink. That could have sunk his career. And eventually would, if he didn't get a handle on it.

There was Alcoholics Anonymous. Should he seek out a meeting? He didn't want to, at this time anyway. Key West was a small town.

The phone rang. He saw it was Alice.

"Hello, Sugar. Just got home after a six-hour drive from Lauderdale. I'm sick of driving. Think I'll sell my car. Want to buy it?"

Gleason smiled.

"No, actually thinking of getting rid of mine."

"Guess you'd like to hear about what happened in Bradenton."

Gleason got up from the chair on the deck and went inside.

"Yeah, go ahead," he said, sliding shut the door.

"The cops were on thin ice from the beginning. Search Warrant based on hearsay. Phone call comes in saying Frank's dealing. Sounds legit. They put the place under surveillance. See nothing. Decide to get a warrant. "

"But they did find those drugs in Frank's desk, right?"

"True but there was no way they could prove they were his. And then there's the question of the warrant.

Most likely it wouldn't have been admissible. Bill Lundy admitted he had felt this way all along. He called me when he heard about the disposition. Nice man."

"Thought they had a witness," Gleason said.

"Yeah, they thought so, too," Alice laughed. "Until he was arrested by the Feds for dealing. The guy occasionally worked for Frank. They had a falling out. He probably ratted to the cops. Anyway there went his credibility. Prosecutor decided the case wasn't worth any more time."

Gleason sat down.

"Thanks for everything, Alice. Big relief."

"You're welcome, darling. Guess your sister's happy."

"Haven't heard from her."

Alice paused.

"Really," she said.

"What do I owe you?"

"Nothing. Consider it a professional courtesy."

CHAPTER 19

NO CELLPHONE WAS FOUND in Monica Kuun's effects. Powers had gone through everything and returned the package to the evidence room. She'd even gone back to the condo in Truman Annex for another look around. Still nothing.

But the fingerprint search had paid off. A hit had come in from NCIC that morning. Monica had been arrested once in New Orleans. Further checking with the New Orleans Police Department disclosed it'd been for a misdemeanor. According to the police booking report, she had flashed her boobs on Bourbon Street during Mardi Gras. The city had decided to crack down on boobs.

The address Monica had given at the time of her arrest would not have been one of much interest to visiting tourists. Though it wasn't exactly a place to avoid, you should walk like you knew where you're going if you ever did decide to give it a look. Powers had checked with the phone company and discovered that a Wanda Kuun was still listed at that number.

She dialed it. A woman picked up.

"Hello, my name is Detective Rachel Powers, ma'am. May I speak with Wanda Kuun?"

"Who is this?"

"Detective Rachel Powers. I'm with the Key West Police Department. Are you Wanda?"

The woman hesitated.

"I'm Wanda Kuun. What's this about?"

"It concerns Monica Kuun, ma'am. Are you a relative?"

"I'm her mother. Monica no longer lives here."

Now it was Powers' turn to hesitate. She took a breath before replying.

"Mrs. Kuun, I'm afraid I have some bad news."

~ ~ ~

Jack had gotten a little more information on Billy's condition. While the doctor had said he wasn't free to discuss everything, he did allow that the man more than likely had suffered a mild stroke, a transient ischemic attack, commonly referred to as TIA. He explained that was caused by a brief lack of blood flow to an area of the brain. The episode didn't last very long, a minute or even seconds. It was reversible and could be treated in different ways. Whether any permanent damage had occurred and how much, they'd just have to wait and see. Until then, Billy needed to stay home and rest. Also, it would be good to have someone come in to help him.

Easier prescribed than done.

"I suppose we could take shifts," Derrick Bean suggested.

He and Jack were at the Inedible Cafe. Jack had spent the day there overseeing the work in the kitchen. A new stove now in place. New refrigerator quietly chilling. Sink scrubbed clean and ready.

Sparrow had been right about his cousin painting houses. Only they were tiny canvases of Conch houses that he sold at a stand on Duval Street. However, he'd taken the kitchen job.

He'd painted a mural. A green pasture with flowers from the floor to about midway up on each wall. There, a split rail fence ran all the way around the room. Blue sky rose from behind the fence to a ceiling where white puffy clouds floated. Commanding one wall of the pasture, a large brown cow – divided into a beef chart – grazed contentedly.

Jack thought the Improbable Kitchen would be a good name for it. Fitted everything else about the place.

"Sparrow can do the nights," Jack said. "You work the mornings and I'll take afternoons."

"It's still going to be a struggle with Billy," Derrick sighed. "Wish there were someone we could get."

"Have to be a saint," Jack laughed. "How are Bobby and Ruth? Haven't seen them for a while. You're still rooming with them, right?"

"Sure am. Say, why don't you come over tonight? I'll be out but I know they'd like to see you. By the way, I love what you've done to the place."

~ ~ ~

Powers felt they might be making some headway. Now she had a new piece of information to check out.

The phone call to Wanda Kuun had been as difficult as one would imagine. But Powers didn't have to imagine. She'd been through it herself. That awful moment when hearing the unbelievable spoken by a stranger and knowing your life had changed forever. She could empathize. And in her profession, that was an advantage. Not only to console but to also gain confidence. She didn't consider that one bit cynical.

"Her mother gave me Monica's cellphone number, sir. It's different from the one she had here."

Powers had called Gleason right after speaking with the Kuun woman. He'd been sitting on the sofa – his: 40 caliber automatic lying beside him – wondering how the barrel would taste. The phone's ring tone had snapped him out of his mood. He'd even let *I Shot the Sheriff* play twice before answering.

"Why did the New Orleans police have Wanda's number?" Gleason asked. "Should've taken Monica's when they booked her, not her mom's."

"Guess she didn't want to give them hers. Maybe she was already in the escort business, I don't know.

It's a good thing for us, though. Wanda's probably the last person in the world with a landline. Easy to run her down."

"So where's the cellphone? We didn't find it in the condo."

"Good question, sir. Maybe she lost it and bought a new phone. Or the murderer took it."

Gleason laughed.

"We can get a record of the victim's phone calls from the number you have," he said. "Find out from the phone company here if they got a ping on her cell that night, too. Good work, Rachel."

"When are you coming back to work, sir? The lieutenant still hasn't said yes or no on New Orleans."

"We'll both go see him in the morning."

Gleason hung up, holstered the gun and put it back in a dresser drawer.

~ ~ ~

Jack didn't open the Undrinkable Bar. The sous chef from Stella by Starlight wouldn't be available until tomorrow. He and Derrick had decided to have the man fill in at the Inedible Cafe until Billy was back on his feet.

Earlier he'd gotten a call from the Moped Hospital about his motor scooter. It had been taken there from the police impound yard. They had an estimate he needed to approve before they could start work. He'd gone to the shop to talk with them.

"It'd probably be cheaper just to buy a new one," the mechanic said.

"I didn't think it was in the water that long," Jack said, shaking his head.

"Salt water works fast. All the electrics are fried. The motor sucked in half the bay. That bent the connecting rod. Need a complete engine rebuild there."

"Any usable parts left?" Jack asked.

"Sure. Wheels, fenders, body panels, lots of stuff."

"Good. You can keep them. I'll think about getting another scooter later."

Jack left the shop and walked out to Truman Avenue. It was still light. He continued on to Elizabeth and cut over to Olivia and toward Ashe Street. Bobby and Ruth ought to be home.

A small voice sang as he neared the house. It put a smile on his face.

"Jack," Bobby Sunshine called from the porch. "Slumming tonight?"

"Just checking on old friends," Jack grinned.

Ruth LaVere stepped out the front door, an African Grey parrot perched on her arm. The bird broke into *Fly Me to the Moon*.

"Roy, hush up that nonsense," Ruth scolded good-naturedly, then to Jack, "Better come inside before he takes it seriously."

Jack followed Ruth in, Bobby after him. Memories scattered everywhere. Jack had loved living in this little house. Ruth placed Roy in his cage and went to the kitchen to make a pot of coffee.

"See you're walking," Bobby said. "Scooter's not ready yet?"

"It was totaled. I'm not sure I'll get another one."

"Probably be wise not to. Two-wheel coffins what I call 'em."

Jack opened the birdcage door and stroked Roy's head.

"Kid that took it broke his arm when he ran off the pier," he said. "Lucky it wasn't his neck."

"Sad thing," Bobby said glumly, shaking his head. "Down here having fun and look what happened to him. You pressing charges?"

"Don't think it's up to me, Bobby. Law is pretty clear. Guy's facing a felony."

Bobby brightened.

"Manifest sensitivity," he said. "We're looking at an opportunity right here, Jack."

Jack rolled his eyes.

"Oh, don't tell me you mean that happy recipient insanity," he said.

"Or as the Boy Scouts put it, do a good turn daily," Bobby nodded.

"Bobby, you realize I've heard all this before. Okay?"

"Then realize your blessings when someone does a nice thing for you." Bobby plowed on undaunted. "You've got plenty to work with there, Jack. Then become a happy recipient and pass along those good vibes. Makes you stronger in the end. You could do that for the poor boy who broke his arm."

"Bobby, he was a spoiled little asshole drunk out of his mind who stole my scooter. Could've killed somebody."

"Ah, but he didn't kill anyone," Bobby smiled, holding up a finger. "Child's suffered enough already, Jack. Folks probably worried sick, too. You need to talk to the police."

"Coffee's ready," Ruth announced, bringing in a pot and three cups. Jack could've kissed her.

"Derrick told us about Billy," she said. "You two are going to babysit him during the day?"

"Yeah, we'll have to split shifts," Jack said. "Be better if we could hire someone to keep a watch on him."

"What do you suppose a job like that would pay?" Bobby asked.

CHAPTER 20

DERRICK HAD TAKEN BOBBY SUNSHINE over to Billy's the next morning. He and Jack had argued late into the night over who'd do the honors after they'd agreed to hire him. Finally, they'd flipped a coin. Jack won the toss and happily took the coward's way out.

But the guilt trip Bobby had tried to lay on him about getting the cops to let off the jerk who'd stolen his scooter made him remember the garbage bag he'd found at the dumpster. What with all that had been going on lately, it'd completely slipped his mind.

The desk officer informed detectives that Jack was out front. Powers came to show him back. Gleason hadn't arrived yet.

"This is kind of embarrassing," Jack said, taking a seat by Powers' desk. "I meant to bring this in when I found it."

"What is it?" Powers asked.

"Not sure. I found it by the dumpster at Porter Court. But I believe I've seen it before."

He took the mattress pad out of the bag and handed it to the detective.

"I have one of these," she smiled. "It's a magnetic mattress pad. Suppose to relieve aches and pain when you sleep on it. So what's the deal?"

"It was on Dewitt Pittway's bed."

"Tell me everything about this," she said, the smile having turned into a serious expression. "Start from the beginning."

~ ~ ~

"Stop drinking," Alice said. "That's the first thing."

She and Gleason were in her living room. He'd phoned her late the night before, asking if they could meet somewhere the next day. When she'd heard what it was about, she told him to come there first thing.

"Just like that?" Gleason laughed. "Suppose I'm an alcoholic? Might be a little harder to quit cold turkey."

"I don't know if you're an alcoholic or not. If you believe you are, then start going to AA. All I'm saying is you're not as likely to do something stupid if you're sober."

"Yeah, guess you're right about that," Gleason said. "But it's not like I was showing up drunk for work. I could do my job."

"Of course you could, sugar. But you admit you've been a little careless here of late. And look what's happened now. You almost got a DUI and thought about blowing your brains out."

Alice got up and walked to the kitchen. She returned with a coffee pot and refilled both of their cups.

"Look, stress is the biggest cop killer out there," she said. "This latest problem with your sister and her hubby just added to the pile. You're not superman, baby. No shame in getting some help."

Gleason smirked.

"You mean a shrink. Word gets out about that and my career goes in the toilet."

"That's not so anymore, Earl. But if that worries you, skip the department doc. See somebody else."

"What? Check the Yellow Pages?"

"No, dummy, do you have a regular doctor? One outside the department?"

"There's a guy we used to see when I was married. Just a GP. Not a shrink."

"Make an appointment. Tell him what's up. Ask for a referral."

Gleason nodded.

"One last thing," Alice said. "Stop drinking."

~ ~ ~

"It's been contaminated," Powers said. "I've handled it and so has Mr. Hunter."

She was on the phone with Blake Hardy at the ME's office.

"Where's the thing now?" Hardy asked.

"Sealed in a paper bag. Just in case there's blood on it that we could get DNA from. I've placed it in the evidence room."

"And you say the mattress pad was in a plastic garbage bag when it was brought in?"

"Yes, Hunter is certain he saw Monica Kuun carrying it to the dumpster. He said the bag was open and it spilled out. I've included it with the other evidence."

"Remember when we talked about the six-inch rule?" Hardy asked. "That was the safety zone for pacemakers around magnets. You might have something, detective."

Powers had called the medical examiner after Jack left the station. Now she felt absolutely one hundred percent certain that they had the murder weapon. Incredibly, a magnet.

"There also might be fingerprints on the plastic bag," Hardy said. "They're pretty easy to lift. Lab techies place the bag inside a container with some superglue. They heat the glue and when the fumes settle on the bag's surface any fingerprints there magically appear."

"Maybe even DNA," Powers added hopefully.

"The forensic laboratory will determine what, if any, DNA's present," Hardy said. "Possibly they could find yours and the fellow who handled it. They'll want swabs from both of you. They'll be looking for Monica

Kuun's, of course. We have samples of hers from the autopsy. And also Mr. Pittway's. But since you say the pad was placed beneath a sheet on the bed, we may not find any of his. Or again we might. Forensic science is a lot farther down the road these days."

All of this was great news to Powers.

"By coincidence, I have one of these magnetic pads myself," she told Hardy. "Actually, the same make. Bought it online for my back problem. Got to tell you, doctor, it works."

She hung up and looked at her watch. Where was her partner? He'd promised they'd talk with the lieutenant this morning. Now they really had something to talk about. Should she go in with what she had? No, better to wait. She began typing notes she'd scribbled down while Jack was there.

Gleason walked in just as she was finishing.

"We've had a breakthrough, sir," she announced with a big grin.

Within minutes she'd brought Gleason up to speed and they both went to Jay Halderman's office. The lieutenant was on the phone and motioned for them to sit down.

"My wife," he said, replacing the telephone on its cradle. "What's up?"

Gleason nodded to Powers.

"We now know for certain what killed Dewitt Pittway," she said. "And I believe we have the murder weapon."

Halderman leaned back in his chair.

"It was a magnetic mattress pad," Powers continued. "The magnets would have deactivated his pacemaker. That was providing he remained in close contact with them long enough. He was given sleeping pills to insure that he did. We believe Monica Kuun put the pad on his bed. And more than likely gave him the pills. Well, we haven't yet proved that she did. But if so, and I believe it to be true, then it was premeditated murder, plain and simple."

"I think that's got to be one of the most sinister things I've ever heard," he said. "Hands down the most unusual. How did you find out?"

"Jack Hunter brought us the mattress pad," Powers said. "I'm sending it to the forensics lab to test for DNA. Dr. Hardy doesn't believe they'll find any because it was beneath the bed sheet, but we'll see. I'm betting on both Monica's and Jack's."

"Hunter's like a bad penny," Halderman laughed. "Always turning up. Did you hear the latest? Officer Daniels spotted this motor scooter blowing a red light on Simonton. Must've been doing sixty or more. By the time he'd caught up with it, the damn bike was in the harbor. Rocketed off the end of the pier. Some crazy kid. Scooter belonged to Jack Hunter. Kid had just stolen it."

Gleason felt his face redden. So Daniels was the name of the cop who'd saved his butt.

"The stuff that goes on in our fair city," Halderman said. "Anyway, how did Hunter come to have the mattress pad?"

"He'd seen Monica Kuun taking a large garbage bag to the dumpster a couple of days after the incident," Powers said. "Went there himself later to empty his own trash can and noticed a bag lying on the ground. Saw what was inside and remembered seeing the very same thing when he pulled Pittway off the bed along with the sheets to give him CPR. He took it home intending to bring it to us but forgot about it until now."

"Fill me in, Detective Powers," Halderman said. "How exactly would a magnet kill someone with a pacemaker?"

"Dr. Hardy explained that it's all about distance. Most electronic devices are okay around pacemakers as long as they aren't any closer than six inches. But less than that, you might be asking for trouble. He calls it the six-inch rule. With Pittway, he'd slept on pretty strong magnets placed right against him."

"So, if Monica Kuun was implicated in Pittway's death and now she's dead, who put her up to it? And did that person have anything to do with *her* murder? Do we have a suspect in mind?"

Gleason fielded the question.

"By another amazing coincidence, Jack Hunter discovered her body," he said. "Sonny Breaks was the detective on duty and at first considered Hunter to be a suspect but it turns out Breaks was 'way off base."

"Sonny Breaks," Halderman frowned. "The officer that recently came up from patrol?"

"Yeah, might consider sending him back if they'll take him," Gleason said. "Here's the thing. He interrogated Hunter without bothering to Mirandize him. Put him in cuffs and stuck him in a patrol car to be transported. Told me he'd planned to read him his rights later."

"Hunter going to make a case?" Halderman asked with concern. "False arrest?"

"He's letting it slide. I tell you, LT, Breaks had no business responding to that call. Could've phoned one of us. Next time the department might not be so lucky."

"Okay, I get the point. Go on."

"Two things," Gleason said. "The condo was a little tossed. Some drawers pulled out, that sort of thing. Breaks suspects burglary but I don't think so. I believe it was made to look like that to throw us off. The other important thing is that the postmortem showed that Monica Kuun died from a broken neck. Snapped clean and quick. But the body was made to look like it'd been a sexual attack. Her dress was ripped. Panties pulled down. However, there was no sign of penetration on the victim. No semen. No genital bruising. And curiously, no defensive wounds. Like broken fingernails, scratches, tufts of hair pulled out. I think the woman knew her killer."

Halderman considered that possibility for a moment.

"Our friend Jack Hunter is big enough to break someone's neck," he said. "Believe he had military experience. Knew the woman, too."

"Possible," Gleason said, "but I don't think Hunter had anything to do with it. Just not in him. Here's another thing. Hunter's prints were only on the doorknob coming in. Which confirms his story about discovering the body. Besides, he has a solid alibi. I checked it out. Up all night with a lady friend."

Powers cut her eyes toward Gleason.

"Forensics dusted the scene," Gleason continued. "Funny thing about that, too. No other prints. So our guy either wiped the area clean or wore gloves. Maybe both."

"Doesn't sound like a lover's spat, either," Halderman said. "Though I've seen weirder."

"I saw the victim with a man at a wine bar the night she was murdered," Gleason volunteered. "She left there with him and I was later able to identify the guy. Name's Oscar Boyd. He has an air-tight alibi. He was home with his partner but I'm still going to get a DNA sample from him. Pull his prints anyway. Thing that's interesting is the telephone call he claims she'd gotten before they split."

Powers broke in.

"Lieutenant, I spoke with Miss Kuun's mother on the phone. She lives in New Orleans. I had to tell her about her daughter. The lady gave me Monica's cellphone number. Well, the phone she knew about. There was apparently another one. Anyway, we need a warrant to get a list of calls from the phone company."

"That's brilliant work, detectives," Halderman said. "Stick with it. Guess that's about all."

"If I may, Lieutenant," Powers said, getting to her feet. "Monica's clothes should also be checked for DNA. I'll follow that up with Dr. Hardy. But I really believe it would be helpful for someone to go to Louisiana now. Any word on that?"

"Maybe know something later today, detective."

CHAPTER 21

POWERS LEARNED THAT WANDA KUUN had called when she and Gleason returned to the detectives' room.

"Probably wants to know what to do about her daughter," Gleason said. "Has the ME released her yet?"

"I don't know, sir. I'll phone Dr. Hardy."

"Let me do it," Gleason said, grabbing up his phone. "I need to get back into this."

Powers gave him a puzzled look. Get back from where? She wondered to herself. Gleason made the call to Hardy and discovered that Monica Kuun's body had been released by their office and the next of kin notified. The detective then confirmed that the body had been examined for DNA samples, and that they'd kept the woman's clothes as evidence. Dr. Hardy assured him that his office wasn't new to the game and wished him a pleasant day before saying goodbye.

"Really need those phone records," he said after hanging up. "Get on that warrant, Rachel. I'm going to talk with Oscar Boyd again. Take a swab. Though I believe he's clear now."

"See you later, sir?"

"Yeah, if not we'll touch bases."

After Gleason left, Powers did the paperwork for requesting a warrant and put it in the system. She had a judge in mind who'd expedite things. Then she returned Wanda Kuun's call.

~ ~ ~

Sheriff JT Wainscot had nosed around about as much as he dared. Any more would draw unwanted attention and likely raise questions. Chief among them would certainly be what was he doing involved in a Key West police homicide investigation? Especially one concerning a powerful St. Julian Parish family. Hadn't he warned that Key West detective to watch her step?

He'd been about to take his own advice and back off when Burton Sachs' name had come up. Then he had to wonder why that man was Dewitt Pittway's lawyer? Last person on earth, he would have thought.

Well, there were stranger bedfellows, he supposed. Yet this was something he'd need to pass on to that lady detective.

He thumbed through his Rolodex file for her number. He'd taken some kidding lately for still using that file but he figured if it ain't broke, don't fix it.

~ ~ ~

"I hoped you were calling to tell me you'd arrested the person who killed my daughter," Wanda Kuun said bitterly.

"Both my partner and I are working on finding that person, Mrs. Kuun," Powers said.

Powers had caught her as she was just leaving the house. She had been on her way to visit the pastor of a nearby church, she'd said. It wasn't that she was particularly religious, she had explained, but more that she felt the need to talk to someone other than her neighbors.

"How do I go about getting Monica back here?" Wanda asked. "This is all so confusing. I've never had to do anything like this."

"The pastor at your church can put you in touch with a funeral home in your neighborhood. They'll handle everything."

"What about the cemetery? Her father's buried in Alabama where he was from. Died in a car wreck there. We'd divorced and he had moved back."

"Talk about that also with the people at the funeral home."

"This is going to be expensive, isn't it? I wonder if it'd be better just to have her buried there where you are. I know that sounds terrible but I don't make all that much money."

"Perhaps the pastor can talk with the people at the funeral home. Work out something, maybe a payment plan that wouldn't burden you."

"I suppose you're right," Wanda said wearily, then a small laugh. "Heck, I could even use some of the money Monica gave me to keep for her. I mean, that'd be okay, wouldn't it? Not like I was spending it on myself."

That came as a surprise to Powers. When she'd first contacted the woman, she had learned there'd been a rift between them and that Monica had moved out. But now it turns out her daughter had been giving her money to hold. So what was that about?

"I'm sure that would be all right, ma'am," she said. "Was this like a savings account she had? I'm just curious. Most people use a bank."

"I told Monica that very thing. She said she didn't trust banks."

"Well, a lot of people feel that way," Powers agreed. "So the two of you were working on patching things up?"

"No, Monica and I still had our differences," Wanda said sharply. "I didn't approve of her lifestyle or the people she was around, to put it bluntly."

"I guess then I don't understand why she gave you the money," Powers said. "Was it a regular thing?"

"No, she called out of the blue about three or four weeks ago asking me to do a favor. I said I would. What else was I to do? Never stops. Even when they move away."

Powers noticed Wanda's voice had taken on a harsher edge.

"Next thing, she shows up with all this money. Actually, I felt a little nervous about keeping it here. Told her again I thought it should be in the bank."

"How much was it, ma'am?"

"I don't know. It was in one of those little travel bags. I can tell you the bag was pretty much full."

This business with Monica Kuun was getting stranger and stranger, Powers thought.

"Mrs. Kuun, I'm going to be in New Orleans in a couple of days. May I come see you?"

~ ~ ~

Jack had to make up his mind. The realtor said they'd had a decent offer on the Harbour Place property and the owner was getting antsy about waiting any longer. Right now, he felt like just telling the guy to take it. He looked around the area by the pool where he was sitting. This wasn't exactly a terrible place to live. Did he really need to move?

His thoughts were interrupted by the phone. It was Powers. She said she was in the area and wondered if she could drop by. She had some questions perhaps he could answer.

The detective had been a little farther away from Truman Annex than she'd indicated, in fact. She'd called from the parking lot at the police station. After a very heated discussion in Halderman's office, the lieutenant had finally relinquished and Okayed the trip to New Orleans but on one condition. She'd have to drive. That was the best he could do, he'd told her. Powers had snapped it up.

"I appreciated your seeing me, Mr. Hunter," she apologized.

Jack had gone inside when she arrived.

"Is this some kind of official visit?" he asked.

"Not really."

"Then call me Jack. I'm having a glass of wine. Want one? We can take it out by the pool."

Jack gathered up a bottle of wine and two glasses.

"Thank you ... Jack," Powers smiled, after they'd seated themselves. "I wanted to ask you a little more about Monica Kuun. What was your take on her?"

"Guileful."

"How do you mean?"

"This is all in hindsight," Jack grinned. "I'm an easy mark. Tearful women. Lost dogs. Sucker for Girl Scout cookies. You name it. But I now believe everything about her was an act."

"She seemed genuinely upset over the death of her fiancé," Powers said. "You're now saying you believe she wasn't sincere?"

"Yeah, she laid that on thick. Then there was that phony accent. Boy, did it ever go away when she found out about the autopsy. What was it with the mattress pad, by the way?"

"There's a possibility that the pad might've affected Mr. Pittway's pacemaker," she said.

"Christ, she murdered the guy?"

"Whoa!" Powers replied, holding up her hand. "Don't put the cart before the pony. That pad might have had nothing to do with the death. It's just that we're considering everything at this point."

Jack looked away for a moment.

"She asked if she could move in with me," he said. "For a couple of days. Then she would be leaving town."

Powers leaned forward.

"Really?"

"Yeah, she seemed upset and said her place was too spooky."

"Well, I don't blame her for not wanting to stay there if she didn't have to. And I suppose moving in with you would've certainly been convenient."

"She came on pretty strong, too," Jack said, missing the catty tone. "I told her I didn't think it would be a good idea and offered to find her somewhere else."

"How did she take that?"

"Like it was nothing. If she was disappointed, I didn't see it. In retrospect I wish I had let her."

"When did she ask you?"

"The day before she was killed."

Why would Monica have wanted to move, Powers wondered? And just for a few days until she could leave here. She'd obviously been afraid of something. She'd been concerned about the autopsy. And had lied about why. Maybe she was buying time. And time ran out for her.

Powers debated whether to tell Jack any more about the investigation. What she'd learned about Monica from the woman's mother. And that she was going to Louisiana to look further into it. But what would the point be in telling him? Why had such a thing even entered her mind? There was neither rhyme nor reason to involve Jack Hunter in any of this.

"That's interesting, Jack. I'm afraid I'm going to have to leave now. Driving to Miami tomorrow. Be out of town a couple of days. Need to get an early start. "

"Couldn't talk you into having an early dinner tonight, could I?"

She thought that sounded interesting, too.

"How about when I return?"

CHAPTER 22

"I'M LARRY. I'M AN ALCOHOLIC."

"Hi, Larry," the group said in unison.

Larry went on to tell his story. This was the seventh one Gleason had heard at the meeting tonight. Each had begun the same. Booze had taken over his life.

Like the others, Larry said he'd had to hit rock bottom before facing the truth. Admit that he had a problem he couldn't solve alone. He'd made the decision to get clean. Now it was one day at time. Same as everyone else in the room. They'd all applauded and Larry sat down.

Everyone had welcomed Gleason to the meeting. No questions asked. He was given all the space he needed. He'd been surprised at the mix of people there. Split between men and women, too. Ages from young to older.

He could appreciate what the program was about – he just wasn't sure it was right for him. He slipped out the door as the meeting was ending with the serenity prayer.

Outside, he turned on his cellphone. There was a message from Powers. He immediately called her.

"Where are you?"

"Just picked up the turnpike in Miami, sir," she said. "If I push on to Orlando tonight, I think I can make New Orleans by tomorrow evening. I've spoken with Wanda Kuun. She's expecting me."

"This is nuts. I'm calling Halderman."

"Not necessary, sir. He signed off even though the captain was less than jubilant about it. Everything's fine."

Gleason slowly shook his head.

"Stay in touch, Rachel."

He stuck the phone back in his pocket and walked over to Duval and up to Vinos.

~ ~ ~

Jack had treated himself to a nice fish dinner at Stella by Starlight. He'd taken a small table for one on the patio. Now he was deciding whether to have a coffee there or go elsewhere.

After Powers had left, he'd made up his mind about Harbour Place. He would let it go. Stay where he was until he could figure out what he really wanted to do. He'd also solved his transportation problem. There was the red Jeep parked in the garage of his beach house in Malibu. He'd called his office in Los Angeles to have them ship it here.

All in all, he was feeling pretty good. He got up from the table and left.

~ ~ ~

Traffic had lightened somewhat after Miami and Powers' thoughts had returned to the investigation.

There was Wanda Kuun holding a bag of money for her estranged daughter. How did Monica come by it? Very likely her mother hadn't a clue. She also had to get in touch with Sheriff Wainscot tomorrow. She'd missed his call and had left him a message. How far was St. Julian Parish from New Orleans? She'd need somewhere to stay, too.

She checked the rearview mirror, saw no lights directly behind her and kicked up the cruise control another 20 mph. She had on her driving outfit – shorts, t-shirt and sneakers. She was ready for the long haul.

~ ~ ~

Jack spotted Vinos ahead. He was more or less just taking a stroll after dinner and hadn't really planned on stopping anywhere. But now, since he was here...

Gleason, seated on the porch, noticed him hesitate out front. Should he say something, he wondered? The guy might be better company than himself.

"Hunter," he called out. "Up here."

"Talked with your partner earlier," Jack said, taking a seat. "Told me she was going out of town. Up to Miami. Guess you'll have to start working again, huh?"

"Now why would a sensible person like Detective Powers be speaking with you?"

"Talk with sensible people all the time, present company excluded. But she wanted to know my take on Monica Kuun."

Gleason nodded.

"You drinking?" Jack asked, looking around for the waiter.

"No. What *is* your take on Monica Kuun?"

"Basically, the woman was in over her head about something."

Jack then repeated what he'd told Powers.

"Nothing to make book on," Gleason said when he'd finished.

Jack shrugged.

"Just how she came across to me, that's all," he said. "What about that mattress pad? Find out anything on it? "

"Currently under investigation," Gleason smiled.

"My understanding is it could've been a murder weapon," Jack smiled back. "Put the brakes on Pittway's heart. That true?"

Jack was guessing but Gleason wondered if Powers had filled him in. If so, she'd been 'way out of line.

"Only thing I can tell you is Dewitt Pittway's body has been released."

"What about Monica Kuun?"

"She's free to go, too."

Jack laughed.

"Why are you being so cagey, Earl? You've got two murders. I was there for both of them. Make that after the fact, please."

Gleason turned to him.

"The fact is we have one murder at the present. The other death is still under investigation."

"Okay, split hairs then. But it's possible I could remember something more that'd help."

"I'm sure you'll let us know."

They sat silently for a moment.

"I was about to say 'don't count on it'," Jack said. "But, yeah, if anything else comes to mind, I'll call."

Gleason sighed and stood.

"Yeah, sorry to be a prick. I'm heading home."

Jack watched the detective leave the porch and fall in with the passersby. He decided to do the same.

CHAPTER 23

POWERS HAD PUSHED STEADILY through the night and by daybreak had driven nearly to the top of Florida. She'd then left the interstate to find somewhere she could grab a few hours of sleep. Twenty minutes later she'd pulled into the lot at the Wigwam Motel.

"Usually, folks checking out this time of day," the man behind the desk yawned, openly appraising her and liking what he saw.

Seedy guy with a gut hanging over his belt. He'd come out from a room off the office. Judging from his disheveled appearance, he must've been sleeping there. She'd rung the desk bell five or six times to get him.

"Usually, I don't drive all night," Powers smiled.

"Not sure we have anything available right now, honey," he grinned. "Most of you gals come in later."

"Sign out there says *vacancy*," Powers said coolly. "And what *gals*?"

"Damn, must've forgot to reset the thing," he chuckled, ignoring the question.

Powers' patience was beginning to burn on a short fuse.

"Look, do you have a room or not?"

He gave her another sly, toothy grin and nodded toward the back room.

"Suppose we could work something out."

Powers leveled her eyes at him. The fuse had burned down.

"Shut up and listen to me," she said in a tone of voice that told him he'd better. "You're about to find yourself in a world of trouble. I'm not one of the *gals*.

Get that through your thick head, buster. No more games. I want a room ... now!"

"Have to charge you for a full night," he grumbled. "Fifty-eight dollars."

"Fine. Do it."

She slapped down three twenties.

"I'd like a receipt," she said icily. "Be sure to sign it."

"Number 6," he muttered, handing her the key.

"Thank you and let me give you this."

Powers slid her KWPD business card across the counter.

The man read it and turned a little pale.

"I didn't mean anything, lady."

"You owe me two dollars change."

She left him standing there and went to her room. She'd decide later if she wanted to drop a dime on what was obviously going on with the Wigwam gals.

~ ~ ~

The judge had approved the warrants for Monica Kuun's telephone records. Powers had asked for the past six months of calls. The phone company had immediately complied with the department's request, adding that the account had been closed two months ago.

Gleason now sat at his desk reading through them. What he'd learned so far added another layer to the mystery. All the calls were made in Louisiana. Nothing to or from Key West. Monica must have had another cellphone account or used a throwaway burner.

His department phone rang.

"There's a person here looking for Detective Powers," the desk officer said. "It's about a homicide she's handling. Shall I bring him back?"

"I'll come out," Gleason told him.

A tall man in his early fifties, dressed in a suit and tie, stood waiting at the front desk.

"I'm Detective Earl Gleason. What can I do for you, sir?"

"My name's Harold Gibbs. My son, Charley, was recently killed down here. I'd spoken earlier with your Detective Powers."

Gleason cleared his throat.

"Yes, sir. I'm sorry for your loss, Mr. Gibbs. Detective Powers is out of town. Let's go to where we can talk."

Gleason led him to an interview room.

"Can I get you anything?" he asked, once they were seated.

"No, I'm fine. I wanted to thank Detective Powers personally. She's been awfully kind. I've made arrangements to take my son home for the funeral. I'm going to ride back with him."

Gleason took in a breath.

"That's a tough thing to do, sir," he said. "Not sure I could."

"You have children?"

"No, sir."

Gibbs nodded.

"You said you were sorry for my loss," he smiled sadly. "People always say the same thing when somebody dies. I've done it myself but it's kind of funny when you think about it. My loss. Like I should've had better insurance."

Gibbs looked away.

"Excuse me," he apologized. "That was stupid. I don't know what I'm saying half the time anymore."

"Don't worry about it, sir."

"I don't understand why my son was killed." Gibbs said.

"It was a bar fight. Got out of hand."

"That's not like Charley getting into a fight. What's going to happen next?"

"The suspect is in jail awaiting arraignment."

"Florida still has the death penalty, right?"

"That's correct."

"I hope he gets it. Think he might?"

"If he's convicted, the court will determine the sentence, sir."

"I know people say putting a person to death is uncivilized and all that, but Charlie isn't supposed to be dead, either. He was just getting started."

Gibbs bit down on his lip and popped his hands together in despair.

"I'd like to talk with that sonofabitch," he said angrily. "Find out what the hell was going on. Can I do that? See him face to face?"

"No, I'm afraid not, sir. First of all, it might jeopardize the case. Secondly, it just wouldn't be a good thing for you. People believe they'll get an answer, but there never is one. All you'd come away with is more pain."

Gibbs shook his head sadly.

"I'd better get back to the funeral home," he said. "Man from there brought me here. They'll be wanting to leave for the drive home soon. Do you know when the trial will be?"

"The arraignment should be any day now. Then they'll set a date for trial. I'll ask the District Attorney's office to keep you informed, sir."

Gleason saw the man out and returned to his desk.

~ ~ ~

Powers felt somewhat refreshed but not by much. Her sleep had been constantly interrupted and the little she did get was fitful. And her aching back hadn't helped, either. She'd forgotten to bring the magnetic mattress pad. To her surprise, there'd been a coffeemaker in the room. She'd had a cup while dressing and had made another for the road. Now she was on the interstate, nearing the end of the Florida panhandle. She'd also changed into a blouse and slacks.

She had decided to let the Wigwam be. There were a couple of reasons. If she was serious, then it'd take more than a phone call to the local cops. She couldn't afford the time. Then, she really didn't know if there was a prostitution ring being run out of the motel. Possibly. Or the creep in the office might've been just looking for a quickie. Well, she'd given him something else to think about.

She passed the state line and entered the tip of Alabama that touched on the Gulf of Mexico. She'd be in New Orleans by late afternoon.

CHAPTER 24

JACK PARKED HIS BIKE IN THE ALLEY behind the Inedible Cafe. He could hear someone fussing around in the kitchen. Probably the sous chef getting ready for lunch, he figured. He was supposed to have been here earlier himself but he'd overslept. He felt a little embarrassed about that since he'd promised the guy.

"Hey, man, sorry to be late," he shouted and walked in.

"Didn't know you was coming, hee, hee."

"Billy! What are you doing here? Where's the sous chef?"

"Sent that fella home," Billy said. "Had everything messed up. Boy's got a lot to learn 'fore he's a real chef, hee, hee."

Jack sat down in a chair.

"I don't understand, Billy. You're supposed to be resting. Does Bobby Sunshine know you're here?"

"Sent him home, too."

Jack laughed.

"Well, I can understand that," he said, "but the thing is, the doctor's concerned that you might've had a stroke. We're all worried. So what's going on?"

"Let me fix us a pot of coffee, Jack. Take it out front."

Jack went to the dining room and sat at a table. Billy came in a few minutes later.

"You and Derrick sending Bobby Sunshine over was a blessing," he said. "Oops, forgot the cream."

"Don't bother, Billy. What do you mean, a blessing?"

"Man's so full of himself I figured the only way to get rid of him was for me to get well, so I called a cousin down in the islands and asked him to send me something special. You remember that time Marvin had that bad hangover and I made him a potion? Turned the tide in a minute."

Jack smiled. He'd just started working at the restaurant. Cecil Brunner had owned it then and Marvin Rojas was his partner in business and in love.

"Most amazing thing I ever saw," he said. "You should market that stuff."

"Works every time and that's exactly what I got from my cousin. Only double strength. Put me right back on my feet."

Jack shook his head.

"What about the doctor?" he asked.

"Already been to the doctor."

"But what did he say?"

"Said it was the most amazing thing he ever saw, hee-hee."

Jack didn't doubt that for a second.

"Glad you're better, Billy, I missed you. How do like the new kitchen?"

"Who drew that cow on the wall?"

"What, the beef chart? Sparrow's cousin painted that. Did the whole kitchen. I like it. Thought we could call it the Improbable Kitchen. Fits right in."

Billy gave him a look.

~ ~ ~

Powers had pulled off the interstate after leaving Mississippi and was still short of New Orleans. It was past noon, she needed a break and she was hungry. She also realized she was feeling a little spacey. That hour or so of rest at the Wigwam hadn't been enough. She needed to update Gleason so she'd better get herself together. She'd found a restaurant in a speck of a town before having to cross the bridge over Lake Pontchartrain. It was take-out only but there were a couple of picnic tables to the side of the shack. A blackboard next to the window listed the menu. *Po Boys, the sandwiches New Orleans made famous* was chalked in at the top. She ordered one and stepped away to call Gleason.

"Good morning, sir," she said with a yawn. "I'm just outside of New Orleans. I'll see Wanda Kuun this afternoon and then continue on to St. Julian Parish. I've spoken with the sheriff there. They're booking me a room at a motel. Nice of them, I thought."

She stifled another yawn.

"I don't want to know about the number of speeding tickets you've gotten," Gleason said. "We have Monica Kuun's telephone records. All from Louisiana. But the account was closed two months. She must've used a burner down here. Wonder where the hell that phone is?"

That news woke her up.

"Wow, that's a setback. Should we look at the condo yet again?"

"Yeah, I think I'll take another look around the Porter Court scene. Pretty sure the techs covered every inch but with Sonny Breaks around, anything's possible."

"Good luck, sir. Oh, here's my po-boy. Call you later."

Gleason frowned curiously and hung up. Then he gathered the phone records, stuck them in his desk drawer, grabbed his sunglasses and headed to the evidence room for the condo's keys.

~ ~ ~

Yellow tape sealed the doorway and a new lock and hasp had been installed. The rental agency wasn't too happy with how *that* looked but this was a crime scene in an ongoing homicide investigation.

Gleason pulled away the tape, removed the lock and stepped inside.

"Police!" he called out. An old habit.

He shut the door and stood for a moment taking in the dimly lit interior. His feeling in these instances was always the same – one of determination. He flicked on the living room lights.

His eyes immediately went to the kitchen. He pictured Monica Kuun's body lying on the floor. But he decided not to begin there. Instead, he went upstairs. He was here for a fresh look.

He started with the guest bedroom. He assumed it had been the victim's. He doubted she would've continued to sleep in the same bed where Pittway had died. Odd that they hadn't thought of going through it thoroughly before. Too much focus on the kitchen. Sloppy police work again.

Everything appeared orderly. He pulled on a pair of rubber gloves and got down on the floor to look beneath the bed. Finding nothing there, he stripped off the sheets, exposing the mattress, and ran his hand between it and the box springs but touched no hidden...anything. He piled the sheets on top and walked over to the closet. A couple of garments hung there. The tech team must have left them, thinking they had nothing to do with the woman's homicide. He placed them in a paper bag to take with him. Then he went to the next bedroom where Pittway had died and repeated the same routine and getting the same results. However, the closet in there was empty.

The upstairs bathroom was also clear, its medicine cabinet cleaned out. He returned downstairs.

The place was pleasantly furnished in Island-style but not overdone. Hard to imagine it as an arena of violence. A woman had been brutally murdered here. Left sprawled on the kitchen floor.

Had she known her assailant? The mysterious phone call she'd gotten favored that line of thought. Did she have reason to fear him? He believed the murderer was a man. Women usually killed by means other than their hands, except when the victim is much smaller.

She obviously didn't suspect she was in any danger, otherwise she wouldn't have let him in. Also, the act itself must have been as quick as it was deadly. There were no defense wounds. How had it played out?

He walked into the kitchen pretending to be the victim. Did she enter first or follow? His guess was that she led the way. The killer could've then grabbed her from behind. Thrown her to the floor.

Wouldn't there have been bruises on her arms or back? Not if she'd died within a few minutes. A forceful body slam could've stopped her heart. Did she resist during the takedown? That could account for the ripped dress. Or it could've been part of a ruse. Along with the panties being yanked down.

The body was found lying on its back. Perhaps she was knocked unconscious when her head struck the floor. That would've certainly made it easier to finish the job.

But wait a minute. His reenactment here was taking the same wrong turn they'd originally made. The medical examiner had determined that Monica Kuun had died from a broken neck. Before that they'd all tagged it as a strangulation. Still, she could've broken her neck in the fall. An accident then? He hadn't mean to kill her, just put a scare in her. Either way it didn't matter. When a death is caused by the action of another, it is indeed considered to be a homicide.

No, this was done deliberately. Her neck had been snapped by someone who knew what he was doing. Trained in martial arts. Had she been thrown down hard enough to knock her unconscious and break her neck, there would've been head injuries, perhaps a brain contusion. Blake Hardy had made no such notation on the autopsy report.

And now this thought. Monica needed to be shut up because she had information about Pittway's death. That would definitely put a handle on motive, which until now had been elusive.

He began rummaging around the kitchen. Checked inside the sink cabinet for the umpteenth time. Opened and shut all the drawers. Then he took out a penlight and got down on the floor for a mouse-eye view beneath the refrigerator.

And there, toward the back, something on the floor.

CHAPTER 25

THIRTEEN DISTRICTS COMPRISED seventy-two distinct neighborhoods in the city of New Orleans. The dashboard GPS had tracked through most of them before finally coming to the sketchy one Wanda Kuun lived in. At least, that's the way it'd seemed to Powers.

"Hope you didn't have any trouble getting here," Wanda said. "This your first visit to New Orleans?"

"Yes, ma'am," Powers said. "And again, thank you for seeing me."

Wanda's house was a small wooden frame structure built around the early 'fifties and had survived the floods and storms through the years. Powers had parked on the street. She'd felt the car would be safe there since it was still daylight.

"I thought it might be helpful in our investigation to know a little more about Monica. What was she like as a child?"

"Monica was good growing up," Wanda smiled. "She was always a beautiful little thing. Lived in her own special world, too. Loved looking at the fashion magazines. Wanted to be a model so she could wear those clothes, she'd say. Children can be so silly at times."

Wanda shook a cigarette from a pack on the coffee table.

"Do you mind?" she asked, lighting up.

"It's fine," Powers lied.

"I'm not a particularly religious person but I always tried to teach my child what was right," Wanda said, taking a drag and exhaling through her nose. "Not that I got any help from my husband."

"You and he divorced, I understand," Powers said. "How old was Monica then?"

"Oh, she was in high school. Don't think it bothered her none. I can tell you it sure didn't bother me any when he walked out. No love lost there. That ship had sailed long ago. The way I saw it was I could start living again."

Then she took another drag and added with a cruel little laugh, "One down, one to go. You get it?"

Her indifference surprised Powers. She'd seemed to be a more sympathetic person on the telephone. But here was another side. And not a very admirable one, either.

"After Monica graduated," Wanda continued, "she looked for work like everyone else, only there wasn't all that much available. You needed a college degree to even get a job answering phones. High school diploma put you in line for maybe bagging groceries. She was lucky and got a job at the department store selling cosmetics."

"You said Monica's father died in a car accident, I believe."

"Ran into a telephone pole. Probably drinking. He never learned. Thank God he didn't kill anybody else. Probably gotten sued if he had."

Did he drink at home, Powers wondered? Was that what had come between them? How might it have affected Monica?

"I imagine Monica must have been upset about losing her dad. Because even though he'd walked out, he was still alive."

Wanda shrugged.

"I don't know really. She was never emotional. Well, she never showed it if something bothered her. Probably got that from her dad's side of the family. Besides, she was excited about going to modeling school. She did wonder if we should go to the funeral. I told her not to worry. Her classes were about to start anyway, so she was fine with that."

Powers put her hand to her mouth and politely coughed.

"Did that work out for her?" she asked. "The modeling school?"

"Well, I told her she'd better make it work out because the damn thing sure cost enough," Wanda laughed. "Actually, the school taught more than just learning how to walk down the runway. She also took some acting classes. Going to be the famous actress. Got a role in a couple of plays they put on there. About as far as that career ever got. They gave her this little certificate when she'd graduated. She had it framed and put it on the wall in her room like it was a real college degree or something."

Powers nodded with a sad smile.

"Afterwards, she did some fashion shows at the department stores. Didn't pay hardly anything but then she started getting work at business conventions," Wanda continued. "Talent agency got her those jobs. Pay was much better. Got to travel around some, too."

"She was still living here?"

"She was until I heard those business meetings had more to do with monkey business than anything else. I confronted her. We had a big fight and she decided to move out. Probably time for her to be on her own anyway. Frankly, I thought she'd have been married by then."

"Did she ever talk about getting married?" Powers asked. "Ever mention anyone special she was seeing?"

"No, she was having too much fun being single, I guess. We didn't see each other all that often. She'd call every now and then. But she had her own life. You're only young once, I always say."

Powers paused.

"But had there been someone special, do you think she would have let you know?"

"I suppose. But like I said, we didn't see each other much."

"When we last spoke," Powers said, "you mentioned her giving you a large amount of money to hold. How much was it?"

"It's at the bank."

"Didn't the bank give you a deposit slip?"

"I put it in a safe deposit box."

"Where do you think Monica got the money? I believe you said it was a travel bag full of cash. That sounds like quite a bit."

Wanda crossed her arms and leaned back.

"Like I told you, I didn't count it," she said firmly. "Maybe it was tips from the business conventions. You know how those convention people spend."

Powers decided to move on and perhaps come back to the money.

"Does the name Dewitt Pittway mean anything to you?" she asked.

Wanda frowned.

"I can't recall ever hearing it," she said. "Certainly no one I know. Who is he?"

"Just someone Monica may have known that we're curious about. That talent agency she used, do you have its name?"

"Monica told me but I can't remember what it was for the life of me. Some place over in the French Quarter, I think she said. Didn't write it down."

"Is that where she lived? In the French Quarter?"

"She did live there but she moved. Told me she had a new place last time she was here."

"And she didn't give you the address?" Powers asked incredulously. "I mean, you didn't want to know?"

"None of my business. She was a big girl."

The woman was unbelievably cold, Powers thought. Monica must have inherited something from her mom's side of the family, too. Well, she would find that apartment, if it still existed.

"We believe Monica changed her telephone number," Powers said. "Did she call you with the new one?"

"Never said anything to me about a new number. Suppose you could get it from information."

"I know this is private but have you made arrangements for Monica?" Powers asked.

"Yes, she's going to be cremated. There's a place in Miami that does that. Whole lot better than having her sent here."

Powers couldn't help but think a whole lot cheaper, too. She thanked Wanda for her time and left with more questions than she'd arrived with.

~ ~ ~

Gleason was back at the police station. He'd gotten Monica Kuun's effects from the evidence room and had just finished going through them. And in her purse was a duplicate of the object he'd found beneath the refrigerator. A key to the condo.

Did it have any significance in the murder investigation? The key could've been there for some time. Lost by an earlier renter.

He'd compared it with the one in the purse, being careful not to smear any latent prints it might have. But again, would it relate to this case?

The key had a brass tag naming the realtor. Its office was just a short drive from the police station. He was about to get up when another thought occurred, though it'd be a long shot.

He called forensics and scheduled another sweep of the condo. Only this time, they would check for prints in every square inch of the damn place. Then he left for the realtor.

~ ~ ~

"This has to do with one of your rentals in Porter Court," Gleason said to the receptionist. "Perhaps you can help me."

"We have only one rental there," she smiled.

"Then that makes it easy," Gleason smiled back. "How many keys do you normally give out?"

"Usually two unless they need more. But they have to pay for any they lose."

"Does that often happen? Keys are lost?"

"Not really. People are pretty careful."

"What about the last renters? They turn in all the keys?"

"I don't know. You'll have to ask the agent. He's gone for today. You could probably reach him at home."

~ ~ ~

Powers had driven into the bayou country. Bonnet wasn't too much farther but the lack of sleep was catching up. She'd hoped to talk to the sheriff tonight but she just wasn't sure she could make it. She pulled over and called him.

"Where are you now?" JT asked.

"Think I saw a sign saying Garden City," Powers told him.

"Well, if you can make it to Cleopus, you can probably find a motel. But Raquelle Harbor's just down the road from there. I've got you a reservation at the Belle Helen Inn. Elgin Whitmarsh's the manager and he's expecting you."

"I certainly don't want to disappoint Mr. Whitmarsh," Powers laughed. "I'll push on. See you tomorrow morning, Sheriff Wainscot."

Powers hung up and popped open another power drink.

CHAPTER 26

JACK HAD LEFT BILLY at the restaurant and gone home. He couldn't help but cut his eyes toward the condo as he'd walked past, the new padlock on its door seemingly adding a somber footnote to the already grim scene.

Inside, he went straight to the refrigerator for a beer. He spotted the half-full bottle of wine he'd shared with Rachel Powers. He wondered how she was doing in Miami. Nice lady. Attractive, too.

He changed his mind about the beer and went back outside. Now completely at a loose end, he decided to take a walk.

There'd been this floating anxiety hovering lately. Tomorrow was his birthday but he'd never paid that much attention. Actually, it seemed like he'd just had one. Maybe racking up the years was starting to bother him.

He was soon at the Key West Bight. Here he had to make a decision. Turn left or right. Left would take him to the Tiki Bar at the Galleon. Right went around by Schooner Wharf. While he was considering the options, he noticed a trim sailboat berthed at a pier across the bight. He squinted to better take it in. Then his mouth fell open.

It was the *Justice*.

The striking sloop was owned and skippered by Astrid Kelly, who was pretty striking herself. She'd once been a witchy woman in Jack's life but he hadn't seen her for some time. He turned away before he was drawn any closer.

~ ~ ~

"Welcome to the Belle Helen Inn," Elgin Whitmarsh grinned. "Are you with the newspaper or television?"

"Sorry?" Powers answered.

"Sheriff Wainscot mentioned you were here to do some interviews. If there's anything I can help you with just let me know."

Powers smiled.

"Thank you very much. I'll keep that in mind."

"No problem," Elgin grinned again. "Some folks can be a little peculiar with strangers. You take Crawly Wiggens, for instance before he got himself killed. Now there was an odd fellow if ever there was one. Then there's crazy old Herb Trotter..."

"Thank you, Mr. Whitmarsh," Powers interrupted, "but I'm kind of tired right now. Perhaps I could just have my key?"

"Certainly," Elgin huffed.

"It's been a long drive today," Powers said.

The room was nothing fancy but it was clean. She ran the water in the bathroom sink, which immediately came up hot. Good sign. She flicked off the television that'd been tuned to an FM music channel and sat on the bed. She patted the mattress and it seemed firm enough. She stretched out for only a moment. And awoke in the same position the next morning.

~ ~ ~

Jack's sleep hadn't been restful. Disturbing dreams emerging from repressed trauma would awaken him the minute he'd drop off. Moments of unbridled fear. Rattles of gunfire. Weirdest and most upsetting were the smells of battle locked in memory and reopened. He'd never suffered from PTSD. Yeah, tell that to last night.

"Good morning," he said to the dock master at the bight. "Wonder if you could tell me when the Justice arrived? She's berthed on pier D."

"Came in day before yesterday."

"Astrid Kelly still the captain?"

"That's who signed in."

"Say when she's leaving?"

"Supposed to be today."

Jack thanked the man and walked to Harpoon Harry's for breakfast. He caught himself just before entering the restaurant. This was one of Astrid's favorite places. Is that why he'd come here?

He pushed through the door.

A few people sat at the counter. Most of the booths were full. He checked the back area and saw no one he knew. He grabbed a stool at the counter and picked up a menu.

Another one of Astrid's favorite places was right down the street at Pepe's, where she was presently enjoying a mimosa before ordering.

~ ~ ~

"Sheriff Wainscot should be here any minute," Ann Creely said. "How's your room?"

"It knocked me out," Powers said. "Don't remember a thing from the moment I sat on the bed until I awoke this morning. No, it's fine and thank you for making the arrangements."

She had on the pantsuit and blouse she'd worn the day before. It'd been looking a little road-weary, but there'd been an iron in her room and she'd pressed out most the wrinkles.

"Guess you met Elgin?"

"Mr. Whitmarsh checked me in."

"Probably checked you *out* while he was at it, too," Ann said. "Don't worry. He's harmless."

Powers laughed.

"I noticed he does like to talk," she said.

"Biggest gossip in St. Julian. If you want to know whose dirty laundry is hanging out, Elgin will gladly tell you. Think I just heard JT's car pull into the lot."

~ ~ ~

Gleason's call to the rental agent had gone to voice mail. He'd left a message for the man to call him back. He'd tried again later from home and had gotten the same results. He'd then left another message stating that it was important that he get in touch, only this time using his deadliest police voice.

His phone sang.

"Good morning, detective," the agent said breezily. "Al Rubin at Reef Realty. Sorry to have missed you last night."

"I understand you're the agent for the condo in Porter Court," he said, skipping the niceties.

"You calling to rent it, detective? Just kidding. Yeah, I'm the agent."

Gleason paused.

"I'm calling you regarding a homicide investigation, sir. And before we go any further, let me remind you that it is something we take very seriously here. I would advise you to do the same."

"It was just a bad joke. Sorry."

"Murder's nothing to joke about, sir. There are a couple questions I have about that rental."

"Hold on a second, detective, while I pull up the contract," Rubin said. "Toni took the call and wrote up the rental agreement. She recently joined us. We've given her Porter Court to handle on her own. Excellent training. Ah, here's the contract. Strange seeing the woman's name after what happened."

"Whose name?" Gleason asked.

"Monica Kuun. She rented the condo for Mr. Pittway. Sad about him having a heart attack. And to be so young."

"Dewitt Pittway was seventy years old," Gleason said.

"You're kidding," Rubin laughed. "Seventy? I don't mean to joke about this, detective, but I hope I look that great when I'm that old."

Gleason was completely puzzled.

"I don't think we're talking about the same person," he said. "Did you actually see Pittway?"

"Yeah, he came in to pick up the keys. Said they had a taxi waiting and seemed in a hurry. Toni offered to drive them to the condo but he told her not to bother."

"Was Monica Kuun with him?"

"Mr. Pittway said she was in the taxi."

"Was there anyone else with her?"

"I didn't go out to see."

"Exactly what *did* he look like? Your young Mr. Pittway, that is."

"Kind of tall. Dark hair. Good shape, probably worked out. Had on sunglasses, so I couldn't see much more."

"And you didn't ask for any identification?"

"Didn't think it was necessary. Actually, I thought Toni knew him."

"The keys to the condo," Gleason said. "How many did she give them?"

"Two. That's normally what we hand out."

"I'd like to talk with Toni," Gleason said. "When will she be in?"

"She's off today but I can give you her phone number."

~ ~ ~

"Other than for Ann Creely and myself, no one else here knows you're a police officer," JT said. "Probably should just keep it that way."

Powers was in the sheriff's office. He'd dressed in civilian clothes this morning.

"People are liable to come up with all sorts of theories once they hear a homicide detective's investigating the Pittways," he laughed.

"Elgin Whitmarsh thinks I'm a news reporter, sir," Powers said. "According to Ann, he's probably told half the state by now. Anyway, Judd Pittway has met me before so that particular cat's out of the bag. By the way, sir, I'm armed. I hope that's okay."

"Everybody down here carries a gun these days," JT said. "Of course it's okay. You're a sworn peace officer. Judd the only person you plan to see?"

"At the beginning he was. My partner and I considered that he was possibly involved. Not quite a person of interest and certainly not a prime suspect but something. But now, after talking with the victim's mother, I don't know. There could be others."

"Well, Dewitt's funeral is tomorrow. Maybe you can get with Judd afterwards. Unless you want to call him today."

"You know, I wouldn't mind attending that funeral, sir," Powers said thoughtfully. "I'll stay in the background."

"Shouldn't be a problem. We'll both go and if anyone there sticks his nose in, I'll say you're Nancy's cousin visiting from out of town. She's the lady I live with."

"What does she do? Is she with your department?"

"She's an artist. We can run by her studio later and I'll introduce you."

"I'd love that. I need to go back to my room and make some calls. When would you like to meet?"

"Why don't you come back here around noon? Nancy can join us for lunch. I'd pick you up, except Elgin would be sure to make something out of it."

CHAPTER 27

JACK HAD RETURNED TO HIS CONDO and was futzing around straightening things up. Marking time, mainly. Today was his birthday. He'd be glad when it was over. He went outside to the pool.

~ ~ ~

"I appreciate your seeing me," Gleason said.

"I was about to leave, detective," Toni Robinson told him. "I'm glad you could wait until I'd returned. The instructor's kind of fussy about delays."

They were at Garrison Bight. Gleason had offered to come there. A break by the water appealed to him. Also, he preferred to talk face-to-face.

"Happy to accommodate," Gleason said. "How long have you been taking sailing lessons?"

"Little over four weeks. A girlfriend put me onto it. Do you sail?"

"Total landlubber. But I like watching."

Toni appeared to be in her late twenties.

"Your husband sail, too?" he asked.

"I'm not married."

Gleason filed that away.

"I just have a few questions about the Porter Court rental," he said. "As I understand it, one person picked up two keys from you at your office, is that right?"

"Yes, Al was on the phone when the client came in. Since I made the sale, he let me handle the final paperwork."

"And the man you gave the keys to, did he identity himself?"

"He didn't actually show any identification, like a driver's license," Toni said cautiously. "I just assumed he was Monica Kuun's friend, Mr. Pittway. Also guessed Al had covered it. That wasn't a good idea, huh?"

"Not to worry. But he was alone. The lady didn't come in with him?"

"He was by himself. I offered to drive them to the condo, but he said he had transportation waiting and was in a big hurry."

Nothing new so far, Gleason thought.

"Do you recall what the gentleman looked like?" he asked. "Young? Old?"

"He was wearing sunglasses. Really nice ones, too. I couldn't tell much. Not old. Had dark hair, an expensive cut. My girlfriend is a hairdresser so I pick up on hair styles. One thing was funny. He had on a business suit. Well, not the whole thing but the pants and a shirt and tie. Guess he left the jacket in the car. Nobody in his right mind wears a suit down here this time of year."

"What about that suit, well, the pants anyway," Gleason asked. "Did it look expensive, too? I'm just trying to get a fix on this guy."

"It could've been now that I think about it. The pants were pinstriped, I know that, and probably made from a nice material. The tie was beautiful, though. Red silk. Had to have cost a bundle."

Gleason's mystery man was beginning to take shape. Sharp dresser. Maybe in his thirties, early forties at the most. Could be a professional person. Doctor. Lawyer.

"When he spoke, could you detect any accent?" he asked.

"A little southern but nothing special. More smooth than anything. I didn't have any trouble understanding him. You can't say that for a lot of folks who come in here from out of town."

"One more thing," Gleason said, "you wouldn't happen to have seen the taxi he was in, would you?"

"Why, yes, I did. Only it wasn't a taxi. I walked to the door after he'd left. Just curious, you know. He got in a van. When he said they had transportation, see, I assumed he meant a taxi."

"Got in a van," Gleason repeated.

"Like a courtesy thing the hotels use," Toni added. "I couldn't see any name on the door, though."

"Do you recall what color it was?"

"Plain white."

Why would they have been in a hotel courtesy van when they weren't going to a hotel, Gleason wondered? The obvious answer hit him. The van belonged to a business at the airport.

~ ~ ~

Blue Sky Service was one of the fixed base operations at Key West airport. A couple rows of general aviation airplanes were parked on the ramp in front of the large hanger. Gleason stood there with Bob Dean next to a Cessna jet. Dean, a retired airline pilot, owned the company and had given Gleason a tour.

"This is our transient area," he told him. "We also offer hanger parking but the airplane you're talking about was only here for a few hours. Shall we continue back inside? This sun's getting kind of fierce out here."

They went to the air-conditioned pilots lounge off the hanger.

"Yeah, I remember that plane because it was a new Piper M600," he said. "Hadn't had one here before. Take you halfway across the country before you have to find a gas station."

"The passengers," Gleason said. "There were three?"

"That's correct," Dean nodded. "Two men and a lady. Eddie took them to wherever they were going in

171

the van. Saves the hassle of waiting in the taxi line at the main terminal."

"Did you talk with them? Any kind of conversation?"

"Just to welcome them to Key West. Frankly, they weren't all that talkative. Did jawbone some with the pilot about his airplane after they'd gone. Told me the older man owned it. He'd flown 'em down here because the regular pilot was busy."

"Is Eddie around?"

"I'll get him, if we're finished here."

~ ~ ~

"Thought we'd try Ocie's," JT said. "Probably have some decent crab cakes. Season's still in."

Ocie's was a roadhouse set on the outskirts of town. It'd been named after the owner's brother, who'd been shot and killed during a robbery attempt some years back.

JT had picked up Powers at her motel and they were on the way to Nancy Lingo's studio to get her. He'd had to borrow Ann Creely's car after realizing he'd driven the Corvette to work that morning.

"Here's Nancy's place," he said,

It was a single-story building with a brick front. The bricks had been sandblasted to a rosy red and the wood trim around the small display window was glossy black, including the door, which held a tasteful brass plate introducing the gallery. This had all been a recent renovation following Nancy's new success in selling her paintings and at the advice of her savvy New Orlean's representative, Lena Blasko. JT had thought it was a bit much but was savvy enough himself to keep his mouth shut.

They walked through the gallery to the studio at the rear where Nancy was working on a large canvas.

"How's it going?" JT asked.

"Out the door soon, I hope," Nancy said.

She had on a pair of paint-splattered jeans and one of JT's old shirts with the sleeves cut off.

"Take a look?" JT asked, stepping around to view the painting.

The subject was a waterscape in that the entire canvas appeared to be a section cut from the water's surface by someone standing directly above it.

"I think you've nailed it," JT said, raising his eyebrows.

Nancy nailed him with a look.

"This is Detective Powers," he said, turning to introduce Rachel.

"Hi," Powers said, sticking out her hand. "I'm Rachel."

"I'm afraid my hand's a little messy," Nancy said, holding back.

Powers smiled and cocked her head at the painting.

"That's almost hypnotic," she said.

"Really?" Nancy replied.

Powers picked up on a slight vibe. It wasn't friendly.

"You okay for crab cakes, hon?" JT said. "Thought we'd head out to Ocie's."

"Oh, JT, I meant to call you," Nancy said, grimacing. "Lena needs the painting by tomorrow. I'm going to have to stay here. I'm so sorry."

"Wouldn't be more'n an hour," JT said.

"I wish I could but you know how Lena can be."

"Yeah, I know Lena," JT said.

"It was nice to meet you, detective," Nancy said to Powers. "Maybe the next time things won't be so hectic."

"I'll look forward that," Powers said. "And I really do like your painting. Good luck."

Back in the car, JT sat for a moment before starting the engine.

"Think I'll skip Ocie's," he said. "Nice little place on the pier at Raquelle Harbor. Kind of touristy but good food. You okay with that?"

"What about the crab cakes?"

"Burger sounds better right now."

~ ~ ~

"Yes, sir, I remember that party. Came in on the new Piper. Nice airplane."

Eddie was talking to Gleason in the pilots' lounge.

"There were three people," Gleason said. "Can you describe them?"

"Sure. One was an older man. Seemed a little feeble. The other man was maybe your age. And the woman was a knockout."

"About the guy my age, what'd he look like?"

"Around your size. Good condition. Wore sunglasses the whole time so I couldn't tell much more. Had on a nice suit, though."

"You drove them to Truman Annex after stopping at the realtor's first. Did you stop anywhere else?"

"Nope, like you said, we picked up the keys and then went straight to Porter Court."

"Did they say anything between themselves or did you all talk?"

"They were a pretty quiet bunch. I pointed out some things along the way. Told them about the Little White House, being it's just down the street from their condo. Thought they'd be interested, but they never said a word."

"And after dropping them off, you returned here."

"Yeah, I had to wait for the guy while they crapped around inside. Finally, he came out and I brought him back to here. The airplane had been refueled and the pilot was ready, so off they went into the wild blue."

That pilot, Gleason realized, could probably give him the name of the third person on that flight. Thorough Powers, God bless her, would've probably entered his name in the Murder Book. He thanked Eddie and hurried back to the station.

CHAPTER 28

"JUDD, THIS IS BURTON SACHS. Thought I'd give you a call."

"I know who the hell it is. I've got caller ID."

"Just wanted to express my sorrow about your dad and set up a date for reading the will. Sure you want to get that over with and move on."

Judd Pittway snorted disgustedly.

"The funeral's tomorrow, Sachs. We're having some friends over at the family home afterwards. Kind of busy here at the moment.

"I understand. I'm staying in my dad's house. I'll drop by tomorrow and we can talk. That all right?"

"Yeah, you do that."

Judd ended the call and slipped the cellphone back in his pocket. He'd been walking along the edge of a ditch running behind his house that formed the property line. On the other side were twenty wooded acres that could be put to good use. Both for the timber and development. He had had his eye on the property for some time but the prickly fossil who owned it had been adamant about keeping it in the family. The old fossil had recently passed away, however, and Judd saw that as an opportunity. He'd talked with Dewitt about making the man's son a deal on the land. But Dewitt had been hearing wedding bells then instead of listening to him.

Well, they'd put Dewitt in the ground in the morning and afterwards there was the gathering at the family home. That asshole lawyer calling about the will couldn't have come at a better time. Nice cash infusion from the estate might give him some buying power.

~ ~ ~

There were only a couple of customers seated at the counter when JT and Powers entered the coffee shop. They grabbed a table at the back and, for all purposes, had the place to themselves.

"Town's a little empty," JT said, gathering a menu and passing it to Powers. "Pick up some on the weekend."

"Too bad your friend couldn't have joined us," Powers said.

"Well, Nancy's busy with her work. I'm sure she would've come otherwise."

"I really did like that painting. She's very talented. Pretty, too. Have you two been together long?"

"Went to the same high school," JT said.

Powers perked up, waiting for the rest of the story, but only a silence followed. When she realized he wasn't going to be any more forthcoming, she decided to drop the subject.

"I want to talk with Judd Pittway today, sir," Powers said, getting down to business. "No need to wait until the funeral is over."

"Sounds reasonable."

"What I'd like to do is have him come to your office, Sheriff Wainscot. I could say that we have some new evidence regarding his dad's death. Wonder if you would call him? Tell him I'm here and need to see him."

"Thought he was satisfied with the heart attack," JT said. "Something new come up?"

"Not sure, yet. But I can tell him about the autopsy results. I'm mainly interested in his relationship with Monica Kuun. They weren't on the best of terms. A little conflict between stories about that subject I'd like to discuss."

"Well, like I told you when I spoke to him at his place, he didn't seem to know all that much about the lady. Admitted they didn't get along. Strongly against their marriage plans. Figured she'd be going back to New Orleans now. Of course, he could be missing his calling as an actor."

"That's kind of my point. He didn't strike me as a murderer when we first met. Of course, no one is a murder until he murders someone. The fact is, Judd Pittway *was* in Key West the night Monica Kuun died. He *did* know where she was staying. There was animosity between them. He could've gone there, had a big argument, things got out of hand. Homicide happens."

JT nodded.

"Okay, I'll call Judd Pittway and invite him to the office. You ready to order some lunch?"

~ ~ ~

Powers' desktop was clean. Gleason didn't want to snoop around looking for her notebook. She probably had taken it with her. Anyway the desk drawer was locked.

He got out the Murder Book.

Every homicide department keeps a murder book on each victim. It's a binder that contains any and all scraps of information concerning the investigation. Photographs, medical reports, interview write-ups, you name it. No matter how small or seemingly insignificant, it goes in the book.

He thumbed through and yes! Powers had copied her notes taken during Judd Pittway's visit and stuck them in the file after the fact. Had she been prescient? Known ahead that something she'd written would be exactly what he was looking for now? He laughed at the idea of that.

The pilot who'd flown them to Key West was Bruce Mason and worked for Eborn Jet Center.

Maybe the identity of that third passenger didn't matter and had no bearing on the investigation but still it was a piece of the total picture.

He got on the phone.

~ ~ ~

Powers and the sheriff were finishing lunch when Powers' cellphone chirped. Gleason was on the other end.

"Rachel, that third guy we were wondering about who arrived with Pittway and Kuun? It was Burton Sachs, that pain-in-the-ass lawyer. I talked to the pilot who flew them down here."

"That's terrific, sir. Not certain at this point how it fits but it adds to our cast."

"Yeah, my feelings exactly. But at least now we have a name for the third person."

"Jack Hunter might recognize him," Powers offered. "Provide a face for the name. He did see him. Thought he was the rental agent."

"I'll get a drivers' license photo from Louisiana DMV and run it by him. How're things there?"

"I'm talking with Judd Pittway today. Sheriff Wainscot just got off the phone with him and we were discussing how to handle it when you called. I wanted Pittway to come here but Dewitt Pittway's funeral is tomorrow morning and Judd's busy with that, so we're going to his house. They're having a boil for everyone at Dewitt's place in the afternoon."

"Boil?" Gleason asked.

"Little lobsters, sir. Call you later."

Powers smiled at JT.

"That was my partner," she said, hanging up.

"Good guy?"

"Yes, he really is a good guy," Powers said. "Good cop, too."

A uniformed police officer entered the restaurant.

"Hey, Sandy," JT called out. "Come here and let me introduce you to someone."

Sandy Bettle had once been JT's deputy. He'd joined the Raquelle Harbor Police department as a lieutenant. The job paid better and he'd needed the money at the time. His heart, however, remained with the Sheriffs.

"This is Detective Rachel Powers," JT said. "She's from the Key West department in Florida."

"Glad to meet you, ma'am," Sandy said, taking a seat. "What brings you here?"

"Dewitt Pittway died down there," JT answered. "Detective Powers is just tying up a few things. Kind of on the QT."

The waitress came to the table with a coffee pot and an extra cup.

"Thing is, she's staying at Elgin's," JT said. "He thinks she's a reporter or something. Wouldn't be surprised if word about her being here has gotten up to Shreveport by now."

"Chief Brennan mentioned Dewitt had passed," Sandy said. "Having a bon voyage party for him at the family home tomorrow afternoon. Putting on a boil and everything."

"Yeah, Judd's making a Broadway show out of it," JT said. "Has invited half the state, I suppose."

"I understand Dewitt was about to get married again," Sandy laughed. "How many times does that make?"

"There was a lady with him in Key West who was supposed to have been his fiancé," Powers said. She didn't add that the woman had been murdered.

"I suppose Diane will be at the funeral will bells on," JT said.

Diane Brennan was the chief of police in Raquelle Harbor.

"Yep, she and Dexter couldn't afford to miss it," Sandy chuckled. "Might be a few donors around. Election coming up, you know."

Dexter King was a state senator.

"You going, JT?" Sandy asked.

"I'll probably stop in and pay my respects. Take Detective Powers along with me and show her how we send off our loved ones. Say, got a question for you, Sandy. What do you make of Burton Sachs lawyering for ol' Dewitt? Something I heard, is all."

Sandy shrugged.

"I don't know. Kind of funny, I guess. Wouldn't have expected him to have anything to do with the Pittways."

"Same here," JT said. "He was pretty upset about how his dad had been treated by them. Blamed Dewitt for what'd happened, too. Tried to sue him. Nothing ever came of it, though. Of course, Burton was still in school then. Probably a lot sharper about law matters now."

"If you ask me, Dewitt was lucky Burton just didn't go ahead and unscrew his head," Sandy said. "Him being the state wrestling Champ in college."

~ ~ ~

Gleason had told the forensic technician that he was looking mainly for latent prints at the Porter Court condo. The tech had then complained that they'd already dusted the scene, so what more did he expect to find? What they'd missed the first time, Gleason had answered.

Now they were inside the condo.

"Nothing's been touched since the initial investigation," Gleason said. "I was here once afterwards but wore gloves. You can see the dust powder all over the place. So look where it's clean and dust there."

The tech got out his print dusting kit.

"I think the killer wiped down wherever he'd touched," Gleason said. "That or he wore gloves. But maybe he overlooked something, so don't be bashful. If you can reach it, dust it. Think where you wouldn't normally expect to find a print. Behind the bed headboards, for example. "

"I thought the kitchen was the crime scene," the tech said.

"The whole damn condo is a crime scene."

The technician went to work and Gleason took a seat on the sofa in the living room. He pulled out the driver's license photo of Burton Sachs from his pocket he'd gotten from the Louisiana DMV. The most impressing thing about the picture was that it wasn't a bad shot. His own license photo was an embarrassment. Louisiana must use professional photographers, he figured.

"Hey, detective," the tech called out excitedly, "got something here."

The man was in a powder room off the hallway. He pointed to the toilet seat.

"Nothing on the top," he said, "but right here on the bottom is a partial print. Kind of smudgy but it looks like a thumb print."

"Man or woman?" Gleason asked.

"Can't really tell. But it's large. I'd go with a man's."

Gleason laughed.

"So our boy doesn't leave the toilet seat up after taking a leak," he said. "House trained. Wonder if he's married?"

"If he was wearing gloves like you suspected," the tech added, "he must've removed them to get his pecker out. For whatever that's worth."

"Might've been an old print," Gleason said seriously. "Could be anyone's. Get a picture of the seat after you take the print."

Gleason also snapped a shot of the seat and a close-up of the thumbprint with his cellphone camera.

"That's great work," he said to the technician.

"Just getting started, detective."

"I'm going to step next door to talk with one of the neighbors," Gleason said. "Be back in a minute or so. Good job, again."

He didn't know if Jack Hunter was at home but if not, he'd stick his card in the doorjamb. After a couple of pushes on the bell and a rap or two on the door, he reached to get out the cards. Right then, Jack passed the pool compound, heading toward him.

"Detective Gleason," Jack greeted. "What a surprise."

"Just the man I want to see," Gleason grinned, adding, "for once."

"Come in," Jack said. "Too hot to stand out here."

They went inside Jack's condo. The air conditioning was a relief.

"Get you anything?" Jack asked.

"Here on business," Gleason told him, removing the photo from his pocket and showing it to Jack. "Wonder if you recognize this man?"

Jack squinted at the picture.

"Yeah, think so. What is this, a casting headshot? Looks like an actor."

"Just someone who might be able to help us out. Where do you know him from?"

"He's the guy that was with Pittway and Monica. The one I'd thought was the rental agent. I've already told Detective Powers that."

"You're sure this is same person?" Gleason said. "I mean, you saw his face, right? He wasn't wearing sun glasses or anything?"

"Not when he came out to leave. I remember because he seemed startled when he noticed me. Put on the glasses then and went to his car."

Gleason smiled.

"I hate to admit this, Hunter, but you've been a big help."

"Any time, detective."

"One more thing, sign the photo and put today's date on it, okay?"

Jack wrote down his name with a great flourish and dated it.

"By the way," he said, "today's my birthday. The seventeenth."

He had no idea why he'd blurted that out.

"Happy birthday," Gleason said dryly.

"Stop by the Inedible Cafe tonight and I'll buy you a drink," Jack offered. "I'm sitting in with the band."

"Last time I was in that dump, I got socked in the jaw," Gleason replied.

"Maybe you'll get lucky again."

CHAPTER 29

JT AND RACHEL HAD RETURNED to the sheriff's station, where he'd dropped off Ann Creely's car and picked up his Corvette. He'd put down the top for the drive to Judd Pittway's house.

"How do you like the countryside?" he asked, as they sped along the narrow road cutting through the swamp.

"What was that, sir?" Powers replied, her hand to her ear.

Between the whipping wind and the roaring exhaust, conversation was difficult.

"I said what do you think of the bayou?" JT yelled, leaning over. "Thought we'd take the scenic route. Show you a part of Louisiana most visitors miss."

"It's beautiful," Powers grinned painfully, her back in agony from the thinly-padded, low-slung seat.

"Judd's place is just up ahead," JT smiled, putting his foot to it. "Be there in no time."

The big 435 cc V8 up front roared and twenty minutes later, they pulled into the driveway. Judd waved at them from the front porch.

"I could hear you coming a mile off, Sheriff," he laughed, walking up to the car. "You should get the muffler fixed on that thing before you get a ticket."

JT shrugged and got out.

"Appreciate your seeing us, Judd," he said. "We'll try not to take up too much of your time."

Pittway went around and opened the door for Powers.

"Nice to meet you again, ma'am," he said.

Powers smiled and mouthed 'thank you'.

"Why don't we go sit on the porch," Pittway said. "Get this over with."

~ ~ ~

Gleason had returned to the police station hoping to learn that IAFIS had identified the fingerprint taken from the toilet seat. Sadly, the national fingerprint database which held more than six-million prints had no record of the one he'd sent.

He was now in Halderman's office.

"Obviously, the guy has never been booked," he said. "Although the print's kind of smeared. Could be it's unreadable."

"Also could be the print has nothing to do with this case," Halderman suggested. "Belongs to someone there a year ago."

"Christ, I just had this awful thought," Gleason chuckled. "You don't think it could be Sonny Break's? He decided to relieve his bladder at the scene."

Halderman couldn't help but laugh.

"He'll probably be the chief someday," he added.

"Wouldn't surprise me," Gleason said. "Powers mentioned something about Monica Kuun having the condo cleaned after Pittway died. Wonder how good a job they did? I mean, if they did a real scrub-down, then this print is significant. Think I'll give the rental company a call."

"Hear anything back from Powers?" Halderman asked.

"They're burying Dewitt Pittway tomorrow."

"Well, stay in touch."

~ ~ ~

Judd Pittway had a pitcher of iced tea sitting on the table.

"My wife made this tea," he said. "She's over at Wyatt's helping Betty get things ready for tomorrow. Just left. You might've passed her."

"We came the back way," JT said. "How is Colleen?"

"She's fine," Judd told them, pouring a glass for Powers and JT. "Be glad when this funeral is done and over with. This is sun-sweetened tea. Don't care much for sugar myself."

"It's very good," Powers smiled, sipping.

"So what can I do for you, detective?" Judd asked.

"As I said, we're just trying to tie up some loose ends about your father's death," Powers began.

"He had a heart attack is what I understood. What's loose about that?"

"Yes, it was a heart attack but apparently something went wrong with his pacemaker," Powers said. "It stopped working. Do you know if he saw his doctor regularly?"

"I suppose so. Doctor's up in Baton Rouge. I can get you his name if that'd help."

"The reason I asked is that when we spoke in Key West, you mentioned that Mr. Pittway might've been getting forgetful. I imagine Monica Kuun would've kept track of things like his appointments."

Judd laughed.

"If she could spare the time from figuring out how to get his money, maybe so."

Powers paused.

"You really didn't like her, did you," she said.

"I saw through that phony bitch the moment we met. Tried to tell my dad what she was up to but he wouldn't listen."

"Funny, she told me that you all accepted her with open arms."

Judd snorted another laugh.

"In her dreams," he said. "Never happened."

"Have you heard from her?" Powers asked. "Since your dad passed?"

"Hell no, and I'm not surprised."

Powers sat on that for a moment.

"You don't find that strange? The funeral is tomorrow. I would've thought she'd want to be here for it. They were so close, according to her."

Judd folded his arms.

"Now that he's dead, she knows damn well her little game is over," he said. "And she also knows how we feel about her."

"Still, she must have left some of her things here," Powers said. "Dresses, whatever. She might want those."

"Then she better send for them," Judd said angrily. "Else I'm throwing it all out."

"You mentioned Monica and your dad having separate bedrooms. Could I see them after we've finished here?"

"Sure. We can run over to the family house. You can take her crap back with you. She's probably still living it up in Key West."

Powers considered telling him that Monica was no longer living anywhere but decided to save that tidbit for later.

"When you came to our office in Key West to inquire about your dad, I asked if you planned to see Monica before you left. You said not if you could help it, I believe. Did you, in fact, see her?"

"No way," Judd said, shaking his head for emphasis. "I had a flight plan for early the next morning. I went back to the hotel, did a little pool time, ordered some room service and hit the sack."

Powers looked at Judd. She believed he was telling the truth.

"I'd like to go see those bedrooms now," she said.

~ ~ ~

Kaye Outerbridge headed up the maid service that Reef Realty used. She was an older lady with a down-island accent and a sweet disposition.

"My girls are thorough, mister detective," she said.

Gleason had found out from the rental office that Outerbridge was cleaning a condo in another part of Truman Annex.

"That poor lady in Porter Court wanted her place cleaned after the man had died. I told her, don't you worry, honey," she chuckled, "they don't do it right, I'll send them home and do it myself."

"So you all went over the condo pretty well, huh? Top to bottom."

"Pretty well?" she laughed. "You ever hear of a deep clean? That's what we do. Only we call it deep-as-the-blue-ocean clean. Sounds like a song, doesn't it? Rugs. Floor. Bathroom. Bedrooms. Kitchen. Not a speck of anything left when my ladies are done, honey."

Gleason thanked her and walked back to his car. He believed there probably *wasn't* a speck of anything left when they'd finished.

The print technician had done his own version of a deep clean. That single partial print beneath the toilet seat was the only one he'd found downstairs.

Upstairs held nothing new. The initial dusting had revealed a few prints around a closet and some in the bathroom. They'd been identified as belonging to Monica Kuun. But this time the technician had gone over every square inch of the bedrooms, even dusted behind the headboards, and in the bath.

Obviously, Monica had been the only person to have used the upstairs area. This also meant her killer had remained downstairs during the whole time and must have wiped down everything he might've touched there. But he'd missed one small place and had left behind compelling evidence of his having been at the scene that was more believable even than that of an eye witness.

~ ~ ~

Jack disassembled his new tenor saxophone and put it in the case. He was in a foul mood.

He'd earlier spoken with the company in Los Angeles that was shipping his Jeep to get an update. Should be arriving any day now, he'd figured. But no, it'd be a few more days, they'd apologized, because the auto carrier had to pick up a car in Monterey before heading east. Worse, they would have to drop off his vehicle in Miami. Something about not being licensed for the Keys. Jack suspected they just didn't want to make the drive down but reluctantly had agreed to pick up the Jeep there.

It was still a little early but he grabbed up the sax anyway and left for the Inedible Cafe.

CHAPTER 30

NICOLL PITTWAY HAD HAD THE FAMILY home built around the turn of the last century after making a killing on a huge land swindle. He'd modeled the architecture after a beautiful plantation home from the 1830s but his aim had been off and he'd missed the mark considerably.

"This place is huge," Powers said. "I'd get lost in here."

"Well, it served a lot of Pittways over the years," Judd said proudly. "Great granddad Nicoll had two wives. Not at the same time. But it made for a big family."

She and JT had followed him in the Corvette to the house. They were now standing in the foyer.

"Did your father have any brothers or sisters?" she asked.

"Dad had a brother. He drank himself to death. Never married. There was a great aunt who was a spinster and lived in Maryland but she's long gone. Don't remember her all that well. Dad never talked about the others. I might have some third or fourth cousins out there. Damned if I know or care."

What a sad family, Powers thought. Even the house was cheerless.

"Monica's room is upstairs," Judd indicated.

"You all go ahead," JT said. "I'll wait here. Take your time."

It was the smallest of four bedrooms but it offered a wonderful view of the bayou.

"Was Dewitt's room next door?" Powers asked.

"Down the hall," Judd said. "His and my mom's rooms adjoined. Wyatt and I shared the other and sis slept here."

Odd that he would've stuck Monica in this room instead of the one next to his, Powers thought. She took in the tiny room. There really wasn't all that much to see. A closet with a few dresses on hangers, couple pairs of shoes in a rack. Some cosmetics setting on the dressing table, a vial of perfume. She removed the glass stopper and sniffed it. Expensive. Why hadn't she taken that with her? She pulled open a drawer in the table. Inside were a key ring and a small leather-bound address book.

"If you want to take any of this stuff back to Monica," Judd said, "I'll go get you a box."

She turned to see him standing in the doorway.

"That'd be a big help," she answered.

She went over to a chest-of-drawers. Underwear, pair of shorts, dressy t-shirts, a lightweight sweater, jewelry box. She opened that. Nothing special. Really, for someone planning a long stay, Monica had brought only the bare necessities.

Judd returned with an old scuffed suitcase and tossed it on the bed.

"This is better'n a box," he said. "Hold more of those loose ends you're looking for."

Powers scooped up everything and stuffed it in the suitcase. She had pocketed the key ring and address book while he was away.

"Anything else belonging to Monica you can think of?" she asked. "What about in your dad's bedroom?"

"That was just the love nest but you're welcome to look if that sort of thing turns you on," he grinned.

Powers resented the remark. She decided to push back.

"Did it turn *you* on, Judd?" she asked. "You and Monica ever do the dirty in the love nest?"

"You must be crazy," he huffed, blushing. "I'm married."

"Never stopped Dewitt. Maybe when Colleen was visiting Betty? How about it, Judd? Good-looking woman like Monica. Dewitt off somewhere. Two of you all alone. Love nest just down the hall."

"That's disgusting," Judd snapped, reddening even more. "I don't screw around. And even if I did, it sure as hell wouldn't be with her."

Powers smiled. She was certain this apple hadn't fallen far from its tree. He'd definitely been stung by the accusation. Perhaps she'd hit on what was really behind his dislike of Monica – she'd turned him down.

"When did you say you last saw Monica?" she asked curiously.

"I don't know," he shrugged. "Guess it was before they left for Key West."

"No, no," Powers said, holding up a hand. "I mean *in* Key West. When did you last see her there?"

"I didn't see her there. I've already told you that. If she said anything different, then she's lying. Thought you were here about my dad."

It'd been a good try, Powers thought. Threw him a little more off-balance anyway.

"Let's go downstairs," she said. "I don't need to see any more here. But I would like to come to your picnic tomorrow, if there's no problem with that."

"Be my guest," Judd said. "Bring JT along, too. Plenty to eat and drink for everybody. More the merrier."

~ ~ ~

"Satisfied?" JT asked Powers.

They'd left the Pittway house and were driving back to Bonnet. JT had put up the top on the Corvette.

"I don't think Judd Pittway was involved in the Monica Kuun homicide," she said. "Unless being a total jerk counts."

"He'd deserve life on that charge alone," JT laughed. "So would've his old man."

Powers gave a snarky little laugh.

"I asked him if he and Monica had ever done it," she said. "Had sex. You should've seen his reaction. Talk about denial. Personally, I think he tried and struck out."

Then she turned serious.

"But suppose just for a moment he *was* involved," she suggested. "Some conspiracy to take over the company. Decided to do away with Dewitt."

"I like the conspiracy angle," JT nodded.

Powers considered that for a moment.

"But it just doesn't make sense now that I think about it," she said. "What would be the point? He seemed happy with his position there and how things were being run. His big problem was Monica muscling in on the family. Still..."

"Children kill their parents every day," JT said. "Well, maybe not that often but you get what I'm saying. Heck, Dewitt had a lot of money and he held the purse strings."

"Okay, we'll take it to the limit," Powers said, getting into it. "Say they *were* involved. Monica and Judd. But not just them. Someone else, too. Major conspiracy."

"That person could be your killer," JT said, looking over at her.

"Let's go back to before Monica came into the picture" Powers continued, excited about the possibility. "Suppose earlier Dewitt had been talking to his sons about selling the company. Judd, knowing how his old man operates, feared he'd take all the money and run. He and Wyatt would both be out of a job and left holding the bag. Judd decides to get rid of Dewitt. He knew about the bad heart. So he and this other person, perhaps someone he was heavily indebted to, planned the whole thing. Monica was brought in as a foil. Afterwards, she was no longer needed and became a liability. Goodbye, Monica."

"But why go all the way to Key West?" JT asked. "Lot easier to do here. Much less complicated. Too many unknowns down there."

"Yeah, it's a dumb idea, fun to speculate," Powers said, "but the reality is, I do now believe that Judd wasn't involved in what happened to Monica. He thinks she's still alive and well in Key West. I haven't told him she was dead. Not exactly sure why I haven't. Maybe hoping he'd involuntarily give himself away. I'll let him know about her tomorrow."

"Could be a ruse he's playing," JT countered. "Though I don't see him as being all that smart. He takes after his old man. Clever, cheats at every opportunity, substitutes lies for truth, thinks highly of himself. Not saying he couldn't have done it but I just don't see him as being that diabolical even if he did have the brains to pull it off."

"I have to admit he was pretty convincing when he first came to us," Powers said. "Cooperative, too. Same as now. A conspiracy is fun to talk about but I don't think Judd is involved in any way. He's telling the truth. However, I do believe you're right about the other person. I'm going to run this by my partner. Thanks."

"Have any dinner plans?" JT asked. "I was thinking maybe you could join Nancy and me at home."

"Sure. If you don't think she'd mind."

~ ~ ~

Gleason was facing another night of sitting on the sofa watching television with the cat. But that was alright. He was pretty happy about what he'd learned from the cleaning woman. The owner of the thumbprint they'd found was missing at the present time but he wasn't concerned. They'd identify him sooner or later.

Mitts meowed from the kitchen and walked over to rub against Gleason's leg.

"Okay, okay," Gleason said, getting up. "Don't be so demanding."

The cat followed him back to the kitchen, tail straight as a mast.

Gleason was relieved that Mitts was hungry. Lately, he'd been off his appetite. Could've been that hairball. He opened a tin of something smelly and took it out on the deck, the last of the sun having abandoned the surrounding treetops. He could hear Duval Street ramping up for the evening a few blocks over. His phone rang.

"This is Gleason," he answered gruffly.

"Sir, I have a theory."

~ ~ ~

Jack had let it slip that today was his birthday. Of course, the band had immediately jumped on that with a big announcement followed by a bluesy version of Happy Birthday. An older lady at a table full of cruise ship tourists had then stepped up to the stand and, taking the mike, gave a sexy rendition of the song. Jack was amazed by both. Her marvelous voice and how any tourist had found the Inedible Cafe.

He had intended to sit out the number but she motioned for him to join her on his sax. And while he was playing, she planted a big smooch on his cheek. Everyone cheered enough to almost bring down the roof.

It'd gone that way all night. The band was great. Every musician in town had dropped by at one time or another. Jack had to admit that he was thoroughly enjoying the evening. Maybe there was something to birthdays after all.

And people were still coming in. Jack looked toward the door as another noisy group pushed through. One of them caught his attention, an attractive woman wearing sunglasses. He smiled at her. She removed the glasses. It was Astrid Kelly, her green eyes radioactive as ever bored through him.

He mind raced back to the first time he'd seen her. When he was a bottle washer working at this very restaurant. He'd been smitten to the core. She had later invited him to *her* birthday party and he unknowingly was to have been her present. That night had ended with a gun being stuck up his nose.

But he was soon to realize that Astrid was a woman who lived only in the moment. Completely self-absorbed and a manipulator who could be ruthless in getting what she wanted. And dangerous.

"Jack, you okay?" one of the band members asked.

"Yeah, I'm fine," Jack said. "Let's take a break."

He placed his saxophone on its stand and walked over to the table where Astrid was seated.

"Hello, Astrid. What a surprise."

Second time he'd said that today to someone, he remembered.

"Me, too," she said dreamily.

Jack noticed a few crow's feet at the corners of her eyes. The years had not affected her stunning sensuality, however. He nodded to the others seated at the table.

"Astrid and I are old friends," he said.

"Oh, how rude of me," Astrid apologized. "This is Jack Hunter everybody. And Jack, these are my friends from Honduras, Lisa and Eduardo, and of course you remember Carl Napier."

Of course Jack remembered. He was the jerk that'd pulled the gun on him. And on another night, they'd had a fight aboard her boat and during the scuffle both had fallen overboard. But the guy had changed. Looked like he'd had some plastic work done on his face. Should've gone to a better doctor.

"Hi, Carl," Jack said, not extending his hand.

Carl grumped something back.

Gleason came in just then. Spotting Jack, he made his way over.

"Came to wish you happy birthday," he said. "Gave me a reason to get out of the house anyway."

"Thanks," Jack said. "Surprised you made it."

"The night seems full of surprises, Jack," Astrid cooed. "First, it's your birthday and now this handsome gentleman shows up. Are you going to introduce us?"

"This is Detective Earl Gleason," Jack said. "He's with the Key West Police Department."

"My, a policeman," Astrid said mischievously. "I like a man with handcuffs. Here, come sit by me."

Gleason started to protest but then sat down.

"Carl, be a dear and get some drinks from the bar," Astrid said, adding. "Won't you join us, Jack?"

"Band's ready to play again," Jack said, wondering if he should let Gleason know what he was getting into. He went back to the bandstand.

Eduardo looked curiously at Gleason.

"What do you do for the police?" he asked.

"Arrest people."

Astrid's leg touched against Gleason's.

"You have a sense of humor, detective," Eduardo smiled.

"Really? I've never been accused of that."

"I think you are being hard on yourself. You're quite funny."

"Eduardo and Lisa are my friends from Honduras," Astrid said, offering another tentative touch. "They're visiting in Miami and we sailed down here on my boat. It's the *Justice*. We're berthed at the Key West Bight. I'll show you later, okay?"

"Honduras, huh?" Gleason said, ignoring her invitation. "Someone in my line of work would stay busy there."

"It's not that bad," Eduardo smiled. "The newspapers exaggerate everything."

"You look familiar," Gleason said. "What business are you in?"

"Bananas."

Gleason laughed.

"Now that's what I call funny," he said.

Napier arrived with a bottle of champagne and five glasses.

"Nothing for us, Carl," Eduardo said, getting to his feet. "Lisa isn't feeling well. We're going back to the boat. Nice to meet you, detective.

"I have to leave, too," Gleason said, also getting up from his chair. "Just thought of something I need to do. Nice to meet you, Astrid."

Jack opened the next set with *I Shot the Sheriff*.

CHAPTER 31

"SURE, JEANS'LL BE FINE," JT SAID. "Ain't nobody here but us chickens."

"Who was that?" Nancy asked, as he hung up the phone

"Our detective guest. She wanted to know if jeans would be okay tonight. Guess Key West must be about as dressy as here, huh?"

Nancy smiled.

Earlier, Powers had made two significant discoveries. The first being that her back no longer hurt. That was amazing because she should've been permanently crippled after riding half the day in that uncomfortable car with the sheriff. Maybe the jolts had aligned her joints. Whatever, she'd take it. The second discovery was agonizing— she hadn't brought enough good clothes. She didn't have a thing to wear.

She needed to save the pantsuit for tomorrow's fete at the Pittways. It'd been through the mill anyway. Hopefully, the wrinkles would fall out if she hung it in the bathroom during her shower. She could then touch it up with the room's iron. She did have a little skirt but the two tops she'd packed didn't match it. And her driving shorts were completely out of the question. So that'd left the jeans, though they were a little tight.

Luckily, the sheriff hadn't invited anyone else, so it wasn't a big-deal dinner or anything. Still, she was glad she'd called.

She poured herself into the jeans and slipped on a green t-shirt with ARMY printed across the front. Stepping to the mirror for a last-minute look, she fluffed her hair with her fingers, checked her makeup once more and saluted. She was ready for the Wainscots.

~ ~ ~

Gleason had returned to the police station, where he'd hoped to confirm his suspicions about Eduardo. but there was nothing on his computer and the narcotics detective had gone home for the evening. He decided to drop it and head home himself. After he made one more call, on second thought.

~ ~ ~

"Detective, so glad to see you again," Nancy greeted. "JT's out back setting things up."

"Thank you, good to see you again, too," Powers said. "My, what a nice dress."

Nancy was wearing a gay little frock. It looked expensive and, of course, she looked fabulous in it.

"Oh, just something I picked up in New York," she offered casually.

Something with a designer label, Powers suspected.

"This way," Nancy said, indicating with a sweep of her hand.

Powers followed her through the living room. She noticed several paintings on the wall and stopped at one.

"Yours?" she asked.

"Yes, one I did of JT," Nancy said.

"Odd," Powers said. "There's a reassuring quality about it. Like running into an old friend. He must be very proud of you."

"Why, thank you. I've always liked that painting myself."

Nancy was impressed by Power's perception and her comment. That was exactly what she had hoped to accomplish when she did the painting.

"Something smells good," Powers said.

"That's a New Orleans jambalaya," Nancy smiled. "JT does it in a slow cooker with shrimp and chicken. Takes forever and a day but it's worth the wait."

"Jambalaya," Powers laughed. "Isn't that a song?"

"You mean like jambalaya, crawfish pie and something or other?" Nancy asked.

"Wait a minute," Powers said. "Wasn't that on the news some time back? Not the song but the dish. I mean it wasn't funny but didn't a lot of people get sick eating jambalaya?"

"Yes, that did happen but it was tainted," Nancy said. "And you're right, it wasn't funny."

"I had a po boy sandwich coming into New Orleans," Powers said. "Jambalaya anything like that?"

"Even better."

And it was. Powers had stuffed herself and her jeans were letting her know. She'd surreptitiously unbutton the top, hoping the zipper would hold.

Nancy had become a little friendlier. She still could not understand what the woman had against her but it'd been there from the very beginning. However, something else she had noticed during their first meeting at the art gallery hung in the air—frostiness between Nancy and JT.

"Who's ready for an after-dinner drink?" JT asked. "Got a jar of white lightening one of my deputies rescued from a still they raided. Rachel?"

"You're the boss," she said. "But make it light."

"How 'bout you, Nancy?"

"I'm fine, JT," she said, and then to Powers, "Rachel, I've got a sketch I have to work on for a painting. I know you all have some business to talk about. Would you excuse me for just a little? I won't be long."

"Oh, don't leave for us, Nancy," Powers said, turning to JT. "Nothing we have to say that can't wait until tomorrow, right?"

"Lena's cracking the whip again," JT said. "What happens when you become a famous artist, right, hon?"

"Lena Blasco owns an art gallery in New Orleans and New York," Nancy explained patiently. "She sells my paintings in both locations, which keeps me busy. However, JT thinks I'm spending too much time at the studio. One could think the same about another person spending too much time away, but I wouldn't."

An embarrassed silence followed.

"I'm sorry if my being here is causing you any trouble, sir." Powers said after Nancy had left.

"You being here has nothing to do with it, detective. Let's talk about tomorrow."

CHAPTER 32

JACK WAS UP AND DRESSED when the birds began welcoming the start of a new day, the evening before lingering in his mind.

He could've done without Astrid's showing up. She was out of his life. Yet, here she was again.

He wondered about Gleason. He'd left with the Hondurans. Astrid and her friend had followed shortly afterwards. Did they all meet back at her boat?

He decided to walk over to the bight.

Few people were out this time of day. It would be a pleasant stroll while Key West got out of bed. He took Fleming to William Street and down to the waterfront.

He wasn't prepared for what he found, however.

Gleason and another man stood at the empty berth. Apparently, the *Justice* had sailed.

"What happened?" Jack asked. "Did you jump ship?"

"Save it, Hunter," Gleason said. "Too early for wisecracks."

"Sorry, I was concerned. Knowing Astrid and all."

"Let's talk about your girlfriend, Hunter," Gleason said, turning to the other man. "This is Mike Green. He's with the Miami DEA."

"Glad to meet you," Jack said. "I'm not into drugs."

"I don't care about your habits, sir," Green smiled. "I'm interested in the woman's guests. Do you know them?"

"No. I only met them last night and have no idea who they are."

"Well, I do happen to know," Green said. "Eduardo Grubber runs the drug trade between Miami and Honduras. Detective Gleason thought he recognized him from bulletins and called us late last night but we seem to have missed the boat. However, I doubt if Grubber would've been on it. More than likely, he had someone standing by with a car as insurance. That's how he operates. Chances are he never came back here when he left the restaurant. Safe and sound in Miami or wherever by now. Do you have any idea as to why Grubber would have been with your friend?"

Jack shook his head in amazement.

"This is all pretty wild," he said. "It's been a few years since I last saw Astrid. We're not friends. And no, I haven't any idea why she was with him but I'm not surprised."

"And why is that?"

"Astrid is all about herself. She uses people to get what she wants. Drops them when she's finished. This guy you're talking about must've offered her something. I don't know if it was drugs. She's only a sometime user. Maybe it was just for thrills."

"She might be in over her head this time," Green said.

"Are you going after her?" Jack asked.

"We'll check the marinas in Miami. Would be good to talk with her."

"You'd have a better shot in Cuba," Jack said.

"That's more than doable," Green said. "I'll even give the Coast Guard a shout. Now, where's a good place for breakfast around here?"

"Harpoon Harry's open," Jack said. "My treat. C'mon, Gleason, you're invited, too."

~ ~ ~

Nancy had worked until past midnight. And when she finally did come to bed, JT couldn't get back to sleep. It'd been off and on like that with him for the rest of the night. He could sense Nancy's being awake, too.

"Think I'll skip breakfast," she said.

They were in the kitchen. JT had showered and dressed, Nancy was still in a robe.

"Just coffee's fine with me," JT yawned. "You going to the studio this morning?"

"Later. That sketch turned out to be a little more detailed than I'd planned. I think I'll frame it for the gallery."

"Not for Lena?"

"She can wait. She'll get the painting when I'm done with it. When are you due at the Pittways?"

"Around the middle of the afternoon will be okay. Got some things to do at the office this morning."

"What about Detective Powers? You driving her there?"

"She might want to take her car," JT laughed. "I'm not sure she's up for another ride in the 'Vette."

Nancy looked at JT, her eyes welling up.

"I'm sorry about last night," she said. "I understand that it's not your fault that you're so busy. Just the way the job is. Also, I was rude to our guest and there was no excuse for that. Lately, it's been so impossible trying to keep up with Lena. I've been a bitch, taking out my frustration on everybody. I don't know how you can stand me."

JT put his arms around her.

"Let's get out of town," he said. "I've got a couple of weeks' vacation coming up."

"I don't know..." Nancy said, blinking back a tear. "Do you really think we could?"

"We'll find one of those deserted islands. Or how about taking a cruise? I'll ask Ann Creely to look into it. She travels a lot."

"Don't bother poor Ann," Nancy said, now in better spirits. "She has her hands full taking care of you. I know how to use a computer. I'll find some ideas online. But you're serious about this, aren't you?"

"Soon as I wrap up this business with Detective Powers you can start packing your sarongs."

~ ~ ~

Elgin Whitmarsh had set out the usual continental breakfast in the lobby at the Belle Helen Inn – coffee pot and store-bought Danish rolls. Powers had opted only for the coffee.

"Care for a little roll this morning, Ms. Powers?" Elgin winked.

Powers replied with a sympathetic smile.

"How is your interviewing going?" he asked, changing tack out of better judgement. "Again, if you need any help with introductions, I know most people around here. What's the story about anyway?"

Powers decided to play along. She might learn something useful.

"Do you know Judd Pittway?"

"So you must be writing about the Pittway family, huh?" Elgin nodded. "Yeah, you'd want to talk with Judd. Too bad about his dad. Having the funeral today. Guess you've already heard. 'Course Dewitt lived a good life. Now, that old boy could've given you some hot stuff, if you know what I mean."

"What *do* you mean?"

"Kind of a lady's man," he smirked, pursing his lips. "Though he favored a certain kind of lady. Kept a string of them. Sort of a bon vivant in that area. Think Judd fancies himself that way, too. Just a little more private about his doings than Dewitt. Smart thing, too. Otherwise, his wife might put a knot or two on his head."

Powers laughed.

"So he's just not as open about his affairs as his dad was is what you're saying? He has a brother, right? Is he a lady's man, too?"

"Wyatt?" Elgin chuckled. "Poor boy's lucky he found somebody willing to marry him. Not the brightest bulb in the lamp. Kind of awkward, too. Still, he's a nice enough fellow. Can't always say the same for Judd. Let's his temper get the best of him at times."

"Has it ever gotten him into trouble? Been arrested?"

"Some run-ins with the law. Even pulled a gun on one fellow. Would've shot him if folks hadn't intervened. Dewitt always got him out of jams. Pays who you know and know who to pay around here. I'm sure you understand."

"I do indeed. You've been a big help."

Whitmarsh smiled broadly.

"We have a cocktail hour by the pool at five to six," he said. "Both red and white wine. You strike me as a red."

"My, Elgin, you just know everything. Got to run."

Powers went back to her room to call Gleason. She wanted to fill him in on what she'd just learned about Judd Pittway. She caught him at the police station.

"So he's a hothead," Gleason said after she had finished updating him. "Could put him back in the picture."

"That's what I was thinking, sir," Powers agreed. "Except his alibi is tight. And I have to admit that he has been pretty convincing so far. Maybe lying comes as second nature to him, however. I mean this whole investigation seems to be built around lies and deception."

"You've got a point there," Gleason said. "Remember that print I found on the toilet seat in the condo? Looked like it was a thumb. Didn't get a match at first. Could've been the condition of the print. But I might able to match it now. I was having breakfast with your friend Jack Hunter and a DEA agent this morning.

One of Hunter's old flames showed up at his birthday party last night with a numero uno drug dealer. I dropped by and Hunter introduced me. I thought I recognized him and phoned the Miami feds. The bad guy had split before anyone could get here. Anyway, the agent said there's a new computer now with an algorithm than can identify about any print regardless of its condition. Offered to fast-track ours. Might hear back today. Also, I'm going to run that photo by the rental agency. Don't know why I missed them with it."

"That's good news, sir. I'll call you later."

She hung up, wondering why hearing about Jack's old flame had stung.

CHAPTER 33

BURTON SACHS ARRIVED at the Pittway family home in late morning. The funeral service for Dewitt was over and preparations were now underway for the afternoon's festivities. He spotted Judd Pittway out back behind the house when he pulled into the drive.

"How'd it go, Judd?" he asked, walking up.

"What do you think of that property over there, counselor?" Judd replied, pointing to some adjoining land. "Dewitt got hold of it sometime back. Know another piece of land just like it. Right person could do something with that kind of acreage."

Sachs laughed.

"Always business first, huh? He said. "I was asking how the service went."

"It went like it was supposed to, short and sweet. You said something about reading a will last time we talked. Is that what you're here for?"

"I came to pay my respects, Judd."

"All right, consider them paid. Now about the will."

"I do have the documents with me. If the family's here, I can read it. Still, why the big rush?"

Judd pushed a pinch of tobacco into his cheek. It was an old habit from his teens that he'd dropped but lately had picked up again. He offered the pouch to Sachs, who declined.

"Bad for the gums, Judd. Make your teeth fall out."

"Yep, that's what they say all right. My brother and sister are inside the house, so everyone that matters is here. You asked why the rush? That other piece of property I mention is behind my house. Might be coming on the market."

"The Weeks' place?" Sachs said, surprised. "That's been in their family for years. I can't believe they'd sell. Are you sure?"

"When old man Weeks died, my dad missed his chance at it. Family was vulnerable then and would've been open to a quick deal but he was too busy partying in New Orleans. Economy's a lot different now. Folks don't have it as good. Starting to suffer. Some ready cash can put me in the driver's seat. Even you ought to understand that."

"More than you know, Judd," Sachs said. "That's why I took title to my dad's place. Kept it off the market. But look, people are starting to arrive. You better go greet them. Let's wait until everybody's settled. Then we'll gather your brother and sister and get this thing done. Just them, too. Immediate family."

"Won't be a problem. Colleen and Betty took the kids to Wyatt's for the afternoon. Things might get rowdy here with all the celebrating."

~ ~ ~

"What time do you think we should leave, sir?" Powers asked.

They were in the sheriff's office. She had on the pantsuit. The shower and iron had done the best they could. JT was wearing his uniform.

"Oh, let's give 'em time to have a drink or two. Unless you're anxious for some of that boil. Crayfish tastes mighty good."

"I'm still full from the jambalaya."

"Tell you what," JT said. "We can stop by Ocie's on the way. I feel like having a slice of pie. It's homemade. You want to ride with me?"

"I'll follow in my car, if that's all right."

~ ~ ~

"Well, I'll be damned," Gleason said. "So you could link up with the motor vehicle office?"

"We can search every state but it's quicker if you know where you want to go."

He was on the phone with Mike Green, who'd returned to Miami and was now calling back.

"Since you said your partner was investigating the case in Louisiana, I went to the DMV there. Guy's print popped up. This thing's really slick."

"Jesus Christ, the print apparently wasn't good enough when I tried. Can't thank you enough, Mike. I'll call Detective Powers right away."

"Oh, one more thing, Earl. We found that sailboat."

"No kidding? You got Eduardo, too?"

"Not so lucky. He wasn't on board. Probably left Key West by car like I suspected. Only the woman and some screwy guy who was with her. Real pieces of work, those two. The boat hit an uncharted shoal off Marathon and got stuck. Apparently, that recent hurricane shifted around a lot of sand. The woman radioed for a tug and the Coast Guard picked up the message. They recognized the boat's name and sent out an armed boarding party. Would've given anything to have seen their reaction when a boatload of Coasties came along side. I'd guess the sailboat took a pounding, too. Water was rough and they had to wait until high tide before a tug could pull the thing off the sandbar. It was seaworthy enough to continue. At least to a boatyard for repairs."

"I'll pass the news on to Jack Hunter," Gleason laughed. "Maybe he'd like to lend a hand."

~ ~ ~

JT and Powers had to park their cars on the roadside down from the house. The driveway and any space in front had been taken.

"Must be a hundred people here," JT remarked as they walked. "And more coming. There's Diana ahead."

"Who is she?" Powers asked.

"Hold up, Diana," JT shouted, then to Powers, "She's the chief of police in Racquelle Harbor."

Diana stopped and shaded her eyes so she could see who'd called. Powers noticed she had on a pantsuit the same as she was wearing but Diana's had come from a shopping world she'd never see.

"Want you to meet someone," JT said, turning toward Powers. "This is Rachel Powers from Key West."

Diana gave her a quick up and down.

"I'm Chief Diana Brennen," she smiled, taking Power's hand. "Are you here about the Pirate Festival? We could certainly use some help. Last one was a disaster. Especially that stupid cannon Joe Tipside insisted on. Well, at least we don't have to deal with that odious man any longer, right JT?"

"No, ma'am, our erstwhile mayor is taking a long vacation courtesy of the state."

"He can rot in prison for all I care," Diana said scornfully, then pleasantly. "And I hope you enjoy our Louisiana hospitality today, Miss Powers. Oh, there's Senator King."

Diana rushed to the limousine.

"Help me out here, sir," Powers said, watching Diana make a big fuss over the man getting out of the car "Who am I supposed to be?"

"Whoever you want," JT laughed. "Pirate sound good to me. C'mon, let's join the party."

They made their way through the crowd and spotted Diana and the senator talking with another man.

"JT," Diana said, as they approached, "you know Senator King. This is Burton Sachs. He's the Pittway family lawyer."

"Good to see you again, Sheriff Wainscot," King said, gripping JT's hand.

"Hi, Burton," JT said. "What brought you down here today?"

"Got some legal matters to attend," Sachs said. "Staying at the old house. Thought I'd come by and pay my respects."

He smiled at Powers.

"I'm Rachel Powers," she said, introducing herself.

"This good lady is from Key West," Diana said. "She's come to give us a few pointers on the Pirate Festival. Goodness knows we can use someone with experience."

Sachs eyed Powers.

"Heard Key West is a lovely place," King said. "Never visited there but hope to someday. Understand that Pirate Festival your people put on is quite a show, Miss Powers. How about you, Burton, ever been there?"

"Can't say that I have but like you, Senator, maybe someday."

An adrenaline rush almost swept Powers off her feet. She smiled pleasantly at Sachs. Wyatt Pittway came over to the group.

"Judd has everyone inside," he said to Sachs. "They're ready for you now."

"Please excuse me," Sachs said to the others. "This shouldn't take long."

~ ~ ~

Judd Pittway and Renee waited in the parlor of the grand house. His sister had flown in from California for the funeral.

"Looking at buying the Weeks' place, sis," Judd said. "Dad should've picked it up when he could've. Might've gotten it for a better price."

"Poor Weeks," Renee said.

"What does that mean?"

"With you, they'll be screwed the same as if dad had done it. Have just had to wait a little longer."

Judd sneered.

"It's business, sis – something you never understood. By the way, how's the hubby doing? Still busting his balls in that nothing job?"

Wyatt and Sachs entered the room.

"'Bout time," Judd snapped, turning toward them.

"Sorry," Sachs apologized, "had to get my briefcase from the car. If you all will have a seat, we can get started."

The two brothers and sister exchanged glances.

"Dewitt Pittway came to me with an idea he wanted to explore," Sachs began. "Basically, he wanted to simplify his will and also avoid probate."

"Hell, I could've helped him do that," Judd chuckled. "Split everything three ways and sign it over. Ought to be enough to make everybody happy."

"Well, that wasn't quite what Dewitt had in mind," Sachs chuckled back.

"What's wrong with probate?" Renee asked. "Might take more time but who's in a hurry?"

Judd raised his hand and grinned stupidly like a school boy.

"Dewitt was thinking of something like a joint-tenancy-with-rights-of survivorship," Sachs explained, "which would indeed prevent probate, but Louisiana doesn't recognize that."

"So what does it recognize?" Judd asked. "A will's a will in most states."

"In broad terms, yes, a will is a will," Sachs said. "And we'll eventually get around to this one. But tenancy-in-common is what Dewitt eventually decided upon."

"That sounds good enough to me," Judd said, looking around the room again. "In common means all of us, right? So, in effect, we still divide the pie three ways."

"You'd think so but that's not how it works here," Sachs said. "There's a simple reason why not. None of you is a partner in the company. Dewitt never formally made you one. Guess that was just the way he felt. So you're considered to be merely employees. Dewitt held title to all assets. Properties and bank accounts. Even this house we're in right now. He's the sole owner of everything – lock, stock and any rain barrels. And as such, he could do whatever he wanted. He could bring in an outside partner, for example."

Sachs paused to let that sink in. He could sense their apprehension rising.

"Then that person," he continued, "now a partner, could invest in the company as a tenant-in-common, and by state law, once he or she put in some money, the partner would indeed own a piece of the ... pie."

"What the hell about us?" Judd demanded. "Aren't you leaving something out?"

"The will covers that," Sachs said smoothly. "We'll get to it in a minute."

"Not so fast," Judd said. "Go back to the other thing. I want to know more about this so-called tenant-in-common you're talking about. Somebody else has a stake in the company? Who?"

"Monica Kuun."

A shock wave crossed the room.

"They weren't even married," Wyatt said meekly.

"No, they weren't," Sachs nodded. "But that affects nothing."

"I don't understand," Wyatt said. "Wouldn't she have to pay him to do that?"

"She did invest in the company. A sum that Dewitt had given her. Enough to put her name on the door, so to speak. Call it a pre-wedding gift."

"Wait just a damn minute!" Judd broke in angrily. "Are you telling us Monica gets a share of the inheritance?"

"Not only a share, Judd. The will I mentioned? It passes on everything to her."

Renee gasped aloud.

"I'm going to kill the bitch!" Judd shouted, jumping to his feet."

"Sit down," Sachs ordered.

"I'm going to sue your ass, too!" Judd continued. "This is robbery!"

"You can take up any problems you have about this with my firm but I assure you that everything is legal and binding."

"Then she should share it with us," Wyatt cried plaintively. "I mean, it isn't fair. We are his children."

"She can't be compelled to give you anything."

"She shouldn't get a cent," Judd shouted. "She's a damn whore! I'm going to talk with her – tell her what's what!"

"You might find her difficult to reach," Sachs smiled. "In fact, I don't think you could get a word out of her."

Renee broke out in laughter.

"I always knew dad was a skunk," she said. "I don't give a rat's ass about his money. Maybe this is all for the good. What goes around comes around, huh?"

Sachs laughed and nodded.

"Little karma never hurts," he said. "And don't bother with trying to sue her for the money. Taxes would take most of it and what's left wouldn't be enough to pay your lawyers. How's it feel to be among the screwed, Judd?"

"What the hell are you talking about?" Judd asked, jumping up again.

"Talking about your old man," Sachs said. "How he fucked over everyone he dealt with. The property he stole when times were hard and people desperate and would take anything, the workers he stiffed on every project he ever did, his bullying to get his way whatever the outcome and always backing up one lie with another. He was uncaring about anything but himself."

He paused before continuing.

"My dad was one of those people he ruined," he said quietly. "On that construction project where he never got paid and never got the money he fronted Dewitt to get it going."

Judd scoffed.

"So that made him blow his brains out," he said sarcastically. "Poor old dad felt he'd been taken advantage of. Sorry to bust your bubble but your dad was just a piss-poor business man who overextended himself. Should've seen it coming and done something instead of standing around waiting for the hammer to fall. Stiffing workers? He left this world owing a hell of a lot of folks around here. Took the easy way out. I call that weak."

Sachs walked over to Judd.

"Actually, everyone he owed after Dewitt left him and them holding the bag was paid," he told him. "I saw to it."

"Out of your own pocket, I suppose," Judd sneered.

"Let's just say Dewitt, with my help, came to realize the error of his ways and decided to make a few amends before his unfortunate departure," Sachs said, returning to where he'd been standing.

"This isn't finished," Judd growled. "I'm getting another lawyer."

"Won't change a thing, Judd. And like I said, taxes are going to clean out the entire estate no matter what. You are truly fucked."

"Now I get it," Judd hissed. "You cooked up this whole thing. Introduced Dewitt to that whore and sat back while she convinced him she was the love of his life. Got him to sign some fake will that gave her everything. And, believe me, I am checking into that. Meanwhile, you're ripping him off right and left with big legal fees. Then after that well has run dry, Dewitt conveniently has a heart attack. I don't know how the two of you pulled it off but I'll find out. I'm going to track down Monica Kuun and when I do we'll see who gets fucked!"

Judd grabbed up the chair and hurled it at Sachs.

"Don't break the furniture," Sachs laughed, easily ducking. "Not yours anymore."

Judd charged at him, fists balled up. Sachs sidestepped, grabbed him around the neck and put him in a headlock. He drew down on the pressure.

"Stop it!" Renee screamed. "You're choking him! He can't breathe!"

Sachs released the hold and Judd fell to the floor gasping.

"Have a good day, people," Sachs said, calmly gathering his papers and leaving.

CHAPTER 34

POWERS HAD WALKED BACK to where she'd parked her car to get away from the crowd and phone Gleason. Sachs' denial of ever having been in Key West was too important – and exciting – to keep any longer.

"It gets better," Gleason said after she'd finished reporting what she had just learned. "A warrant has been filed for his arrest. It's in the system here and should also be in Louisiana by now."

"Sachs is still inside the Pittway house, sir," Powers said. "Something about meeting with the family. I'll arrest him there."

"Take the sheriff with you," Gleason cautioned. "Although there shouldn't be a problem, no need to take chances."

"How'd you get the warrant?"

Gleason chuckled.

"I had the technician search again for prints. He found one under the toilet seat. Belongs to Sachs."

"Couldn't it have been left from the first time?"

"Monica Kuun had the condo cleaned after Pittway died. I've spoken with the maid service and they're adamant about going over it from top to bottom. And I believe them because there was nothing anywhere else, not even a smudge. Sachs had apparently wiped down the entire scene after the incident but he missed the toilet seat. These maids wouldn't have."

"How did he get there the second time?"

"Working on that. I called the charter company and they said that the pilot was no longer there. But they assured me that the Pittway airplane hadn't flown anywhere since then. By the way, I'm sure the key I found there belonged to him, so he could've been waiting for Monica."

"He could have taken a commercial flight," Powers suggested. "Wonder if he booked anything through his office?"

"I'm in touch with a detective in the Baton Rouge department. We'll coordinate with them once Sachs is in custody. He'll be transported to their jail to await extradition. I'll have him call you."

"Do you think you'll be coming here, sir?"

"I'll run that by the LT. Good work, Rachel."

"Same to you, sir."

"And be careful," Gleason warned. "That guy's dangerous."

~ ~ ~

"And where has our young pirate disappeared to?" Diana Bremen asked.

"She had to make a phone call," JT said. "Here she comes now."

"Oh, there's Senator King," Diana said, spinning off and going to him.

"An arrest warrant has been issued for Burton Sachs," Powers said quietly to JT. "You should have it. Is Sachs still in the house?"

JT set his jaw and nodded.

"I'll call Ann Creely," he said, punching the number. "We'll arrest him inside the house. Oh, hello, Ann. Want you to see if there's a warrant out for Burton Sachs. Yeah. Key West Police Department."

He paused while Ann checked her computer.

"I expect there'll be a fight over extradition," he said to Powers. "Your evidence good?"

"He lied about being there with both victims but we have witnesses that say otherwise. His thumb print was found at the murder scene. Only thing is we don't know how he got to Key West the second time. We're checking the airlines and charters as well."

"Look for speeding tickets between here and Florida while you're at it," JT said. "Burton drives like a madman. Has a German car. Forget what make. What's that, Ann? We have the warrant? Good. Thanks."

"That's interesting what you said about speeding tickets. He could have driven. I drove from Key West almost to Alabama in one night. In something really fast and with enough caffeine and a lot of luck, you could make it to there non-stop."

Diana Bremen joined them, arm-in-arm with Senator King.

"Just wanted to say goodbye," Diana beamed.

Burton Sachs, having just come outside, spotted the group and walked over.

"The senator was just leaving," Diana told him.

Further conversation was interrupted by a menacing shout.

"Burton Sachs, you son-of-a-bitch!"

Sachs turned around to see Judd Pittway holding a shotgun. Pittway put the gun to his shoulder and fired. The charge of buckshot struck Sachs squarely in the chest. He crumpled to the ground and Judd racked another shell into the chamber.

Powers started to go for her gun but instead dove into King and Diana, throwing both to the ground and herself landing on top. She heard the whistle of the deadly pellets pass over her as Judd fired again. Her memory flashed back to another time, only it had been shrapnel then and hadn't missed.

The shotgun blast was immediately followed by two cracks of gunfire. She opened her eyes to see JT standing in a crouched shooting position, Judd Pittway on the ground beyond.

"You okay, sir?" she said anxiously, getting to her feet and pulling out her own gun, her hand unsteady.

"Yeah, how about you?" he asked, as they slowly approached where Judd lay.

"I'm good. So are the others. Don't know about Sachs."

JT kicked the shotgun out of reach and bent over Judd.

"He's still breathing. I'll call for an ambulance and some backup."

Diana and Senator King had sat up, both seemingly bewildered. Other guests had begun to crowd around.

"Why, you have a gun," Diana said in amazement to Powers.

"I'm a police officer, ma'am. I'm entitled to have one. Help me get these people back."

~ ~ ~

"Detective Powers is arresting Burton Sachs probably at this very moment," Gleason said to Halderman.

"How's that sheriff she's with?" Halderman asked. "Sachs could put up a fight."

"Yeah, that's my concern, too. I don't know anything about this Wainscot. Just have to go on faith."

"Powers is a good cop." Haldeman said. "I believe she can handle the situation. She survived the damn war, after all."

"She asked if I could join her," Gleason said. "Wrap up this thing. What do you think?"

"Can't spare you, Earl. Colin Doyle's tied up with that homicide over in the Casa Marina area. Kingsford retired last week. You go running off to Louisiana and I'm stuck with Sonny Breaks."

Gleason laughed.

"I thought he'd been sent to the misdemeanor theft desk," he said.

"I'm working on it," Halderman smiled. "Kinda like sending him to juvenile hall since he hates kids so much."

Gleason's phone rang. He checked the caller ID.

"It's Powers. I'll put it on speaker. Hi, Rachel, what's up?"

"Judd Pittway just shot Burton Sachs, sir. He's dead,"

CHAPTER 35

ONE OF THE GUESTS WAS A NURSE and JT had let her through the temporary cordon he and Powers had established. The best she could do, however, was staunch the bleeding and try to keep Judd from going into shock until the ambulance arrived. He'd been propped up where he'd fallen and covered with a blanket someone had gotten from the house.

Burton Sachs' body lay uncovered. Powers had placed her jacket over his face. Several people in the crowd had snapped cellphone pictures before JT could shoo them away.

Diana had taken the senator inside at Power's insistence. Wyatt and Renee had thought the gunshots were fireworks being set off by some of the guests and neither knew what really had happened until Diana told them. She'd then tried to get them to remain there with her but they had rushed outside.

When Powers had learned who they were, and having her hands full at the moment with half the guests near panic and the other half having spent too much time at the bar, she'd explained that this was a crime scene and sent them back to Diana, adding they should stay put.

The ambulance and two sheriffs' cruisers pulled in at the same time. Deputy Ray Wilson hopped out of one car and made his way through the crowd. Two deputies followed from theirs. The EMTs unloaded their equipment.

"Ray, have the men secure this damn area and get a sheet over him," JT ordered, nodding toward Sachs. "Call for more help. And don't let anyone leave. We'll want the names of any witnesses. Hell, take the names of everyone here!"

"Yes, sir. Who was the shooter?"

"Judd Pittway and me."

"What about her?" Wilson asked warily, pointing at Powers who was with Pittway. "Lady with the gun."

"She's one of us."

The EMTs took over from the nurse and had Judd Pittway stabilized and on a gurney. Ron Wilson set up a perimeter and screened off Sachs' body to await the coroner. JT stood to the side with Powers. She'd just gotten off the phone with Gleason.

"That was quick thinking," he said, rubbing his eyes. "You saved both of them. I hate to think how it would've gone if you hadn't got them down."

"Thank you, sir. It was also fast acting on your part, too. Might not have been so lucky if he'd gotten off another shot."

JT smiled grimly.

"Yeah, but I need some target practice," he said. "Fired twice, only hit once."

Both officers shared a small laugh.

"Where do we go from here?" Powers asked.

"Deputy Ray Wilson is my second-in-command. He'll lead the homicide investigation on Burton Sachs. I'm putting myself on administrative leave for the time being. The Parish District Attorney will determine if my shooting Judd Pittway was justifiable. Don't believe there'll be any problems."

"It's pretty cut and dried to me," she said. "Judd Pittway shot and killed Sachs, then shot at us. You've got enough witnesses who'll testify to that. Starting with me."

"I'm not worried but in any officer involved shooting there's always a suspicious eye somewhere."

"Wonder what set him off like that?" Powers mused.

"Judd has always had a short fuse but whatever that business was between him and Sachs must've really gone south. We'll talk with his brother and sister. Why don't you go back to the hotel? Nothing more for you to do here. Think I'll stick around a little longer."

Powers took in the scene for a moment.

"Believe I will," she said. "I need to report for this to my boss. Okay if I call you later?"

"Sure, but *me* call *you* after we're finished up."

Sandy Bettle's car skidded to a stop out front. He jumped out and ran over to JT and Powers.

"Chief Brennan called in an uproar," he said breathlessly. "Said someone had tried to kill her and Senator King. But that the senator was now safe with her."

"Judd Pittway went off his rocker and shot Burton Sachs," JT said. "He then turned his gun toward where Diana and the senator were standing but Detective Powers here was the hero. She pushed them to the ground in the nick of time. I was able to get off a shot at Judd. He's on the way to the hospital."

"I'll be damned. Where's Diana?"

"In the house. She's probably working on her story for the press."

~ ~ ~

"Our cocktail hour is about to begin," Elgin Whitmarsh said. "I believe you're a red wine girl, right?"

Powers had just arrived at the inn. Elgin caught her passing the swimming pool. No other guests were present.

"That'd be lovely," she answered, striding over to the table that'd been set up and pouring herself a full glass. Without saying another word she walked past him and took it to her room.

She stripped down. Her clothes were a mess. She'd have to find a cleaners. Or maybe she'd just wait until she got home. Or better yet go shopping. Next, she ran a bath, filling the tub to the top overflow drain. Holding the wine glass in one hand and balancing herself with the other, she settled into the unbearably hot water. It felt wonderful.

As the bottled-up adrenaline ebbed, memories stirred again. Iraq. An approaching motorcycle. A deafening explosion. Bodies strewn everywhere.

She took a long sip of wine. It seemed to help.

Now more at ease, she returned her attention to the shooting. How it had ironically taken place just as she was about to arrest Burton Sachs. Judd Pittway certainly had thrown a wrench into the investigation by removing their prime suspect. She made a mental note to talk with his sister and brother tomorrow. Then she remembered Sachs had been carrying a briefcase when he walked up.

She climbed out of the tub, wrapped a towel around herself, and picked up her phone.

CHAPTER 36

GLEASON WAS AT HIS DESK. He'd briefed the lieutenant after Powers had called the second time. She'd promised to call again as soon as she had more news. So he was waiting.

He could've waited just as easily at home. It was getting late. Halderman had left for the evening. But for some reason it seemed right that he be here.

I Shot the Sheriff rang out.

"This is Gleason," he answered.

"Detective Powers, sir. Couple of things since we last talked."

Gleason picked up a pen and slid his notepad closer, a habit.

"Apparently there'd been an argument between Judd Pittway and Sachs about a will," she said. "I haven't gotten the full story yet but I'm talking with the sister and brother tomorrow so perhaps they can fill me in. But after I left the scene, I remembered Sachs had a briefcase. I called Sheriff Wainscot and he has agreed to let me look through it."

"What do you expect to find?" Gleason asked, doodling something on the notepad.

"I don't know, sir. Hopefully, a copy of the will. That might throw some light on the cause of the fight. Maybe some financial records that'd be useful. The sheriff also said Sachs owned a foreign sports car and was a hotshot driver. Suppose he drove to Key West? Could be he has gas receipts."

"Get ahold of that detective in Baton Rouge," Gleason said. "Tell him we need a warrant for Sachs' home or apartment. Also, call the law firm where Sachs worked. Yeah, it'd be interesting to know more about that will. If they give you any static, have them phone me."

Powers paused a moment.

"We do still believe Sachs is our prime suspect, right? We have his print."

"No question in my mind that he did it," Gleason said. "The only iffy thing is when the print was made. A defense lawyer would hammer on that point. I believe what the cleaning lady said but it'd be better to have something more solid. If there's some way we could positively date the print as being left the night of the crime, then it's case closed. I realize it's a moot point since Sachs is dead but I want to close it."

"I'd like to be able to do the same with Dewitt Pittway's death," Powers said. "I believe Sachs had a hand in that, as well as Monica. We have the mattress pad but forensics is taking forever and a day on DNA. Maybe there's nothing."

Powers realized she hadn't told Gleason about the keyring and address book she'd found in Monica's room at the Pittway house. So much had been going on.

"Sir, when I spoke with Wanda Kuun, she said Monica had recently moved. She didn't know the new address. I found an address book and set of keys in her room at the Pittway house. It could be her little black book, you know?"

"Run it down," Gleason said. "Call everyone listed. Say you're trying to locate her regarding a police matter."

"I'll get started now. Nothing like a call from the cops when you're home having dinner."

Gleason tore off the page he'd doodled on, an intricate geometric design, and stuck it in a drawer where at least a hundred others were stashed. He had no idea why he saved the things. Maybe he'd make a book out of them someday.

He remembered hearing something about a pizza being brought in. He went to the coffee room and opened the refrigerator door. One cold slice left in a box. He wolfed it down and left the station.

~ ~ ~

Jack was home killing time. Earlier he'd learned that he had to make an unexpected business trip to Los Angeles. Before booking a flight, he'd checked with the car carrier company and found out that his Jeep had been dropped off in Miami. This had been good news. He could fly back from LA to Miami and drive it home. Then he'd decided to call LAPD Detective Laura Dalton and invite her to dinner while he was in town. It'd been awhile since they'd last talked. That call had brought some surprising news.

There was nothing on television. He flicked off the set and checked his watch again. Too early for bed, though he had the first flight out tomorrow. He decided to walk over to Duval.

It was a quiet night. Passing Vinos he saw the porch nearly full, Gleason lurking in the corner.

"Buy you a drink?" Jack asked, joining him.

"I'm good."

Jack ordered himself a glass of wine.

"Hear from your girlfriend?" Gleason asked.

"Who?"

"Tugboat Annie."

"Oh, you mean Astrid," Jack laughed. "No, we don't keep in touch."

"Well, for your information, she keeps bad company. You know how to pick them, Hunter."

"How is Rachel Powers?" Jack asked. "Haven't heard from her lately. Still in Miami?"

"Louisiana. Can't tell you anything more so don't ask."

The wine came and Jack lifted his glass.

"Here's to Louisiana. I'm going to LA tomorrow. Just a short trip."

"Yeah? I've been thinking about taking a vacation in Hawaii. Maybe I'll stop in Los Angeles for a couple days."

"Let me know when you decide. I'll give you some good restaurant names."

"Great. I'll invite your friend, Laura Dalton, to join me."

"Book a table for three if you do. She's engaged."

"You're kidding."

"It's true. Just spoke with her today. Lucky guy's a homicide detective in the sheriffs' department. I've met him, actually. A fellow I knew there was murdered and he worked the case."

"What did that have to do with Laura?"

"She was investigating another murder that was connected to that one. Involved a cult. Almost became a victim myself."

"You're a danger to be around. Anyone ever tell you that?"

"I hear it all the time."

"How'd you let Laura get away? I thought you two were an item."

"Might've been another time in a different place," Jack said. "Maybe it was me spending more time here than there. Most likely it just wasn't meant to be."

Gleason got up to leave.

"Not only are you a menace to society, Hunter," he smiled, "but you're also an idiot."

~ ~ ~

The telephone numbers in the book Powers had lifted were listed with a letter next to them but not in alphabetical order. So far *B, F, D, O* and *S* had answered. A judge, two state assemblymen, a lawyer and a car salesman. All had been suspicious and

236

uncooperative in the end. The judge and the two politicians had hung up. The lawyer had threatened a lawsuit. The car dealer had kept asking if she were really a cop and had tried to flirt. *S* had been eerie — Burton Sachs' voice mail.

Now it was getting late. She dialed one more letter. *V.*

"This is Vicki," a woman chirped in a pleasant voice. "Please leave your name, number and the nature of your business and I'll return your call."

Powers did as requested and said her call concerned Monica Kuun. Two minutes later her phone rang.

"What's this about Monica?" Vicki demanded, not so pleasantly. "And you're a detective?"

"Yes," Powers said. "Are you a friend of hers?"

"How did you get my number?" Vicki shot back.

"It was listed in her address book."

"You sound like some kind of kook. I don't believe you're a detective. I'm hanging up."

"Monica Kuun is dead," Powers said. "I'm investigating her death. Call the Key West Police Department. I'll give you the telephone number. They will verify who I am and then I suggest you call me back."

A moment of silence passed before an anxious voice replied.

"Okay, I believe you, I guess. Monica's dead? Was there an accident?"

Powers knew the truth worked best.

"No, ma'am. It was a homicide."

Vicki began to sob.

"I understand this is shocking, ma'am, but please try to pull yourself together. It's important that we talk."

"You said you're in Key West?" Vicki snuffled. "Is that where it happened?"

"Yes, ma'am. But I'm in Louisiana right now. A town named Bonnet. Do you know where that is?"

"No, I've never heard of it."

"Well, I'm not surprised," Powers said in a friendlier tone. "It's kind of small. You must be in New Orleans, right? I know Monica was from there. Did you work together?"

Vicki took in a deep breath.

"What? Oh, no. Monica was with some talent agency. She was a fashion model. I work in an insurance office. We went to high school together. Kinda stayed friends."

"You've kept in touch since then?"

"Off and on. We'd have lunch occasionally. Things like that. I always liked her. In fact, I think I was the only friend she had. You'd never have thought that because she was so attractive."

"Her mother said she'd moved. Do you know anything about that?"

"That's funny you should ask. Well, not funny in a ha-ha way. Monica called me and said she was moving and would I like her old place? Rent would be about the same as mine and hers was much nicer. My lease was about up so I said, sure. This was a couple of months ago."

"You're living there now?" Powers asked. "In Monica's old apartment?"

"Yeah, Monica moved to a new building near the business area. I think she said a lawyer she knew from where she worked owned an apartment there."

"Did Monica leave any of her things with you to keep for her?"

"She left her furniture. What there was of it, which wasn't much but that was Monica. She didn't spend a whole lot on things. Not that she was cheap or anything. If there was something she liked, she'd get it. Especially clothes."

"Wonder why she moved then?" Powers said. "Must have been more expensive. And since she was so cost-conscious. Any idea?"

"I asked her about that and she said the lawyer suggested it might be better for her work because she entertained at home a lot. Besides, she said she'd soon be leaving New Orleans and going to live in New York. Probably better modeling jobs there."

"Do you have the address of her new apartment?"

"Sure, I'll get it for you. I'm sorry I was rude at first. You never know who's calling these days."

"That's quite all right," Powers said. "I'm sorry I had to give you such bad news about your friend."

"When is Monica's funeral? I suppose it'll be here."

"You'll have to ask her mother that."

~ ~ ~

"Sachs has an apartment in Baton Rouge," JT said. "But he spends a lot of time at his dad's old house near Cleopus."

Powers was in the sheriff's office the next morning. JT was officially on leave but unofficially he was still on the job. Something he'd tried to explain to Nancy but without a whole lot of success.

"We don't need a warrant to go inside," he continued. "Deputy Wilson will run you up there. Have to keep everything on the up and up during this damn shooting investigation, otherwise I'd do it myself. I have the keys to the house. They were in Burton's pocket."

"I was also hoping to speak with Wyatt and his sister today about what went on between Sachs and Judd before the shooting," Powers said. "Would there be any problems with that in your investigation?"

JT thought for a moment.

"I don't really know at this point," he said. "I suppose a defense lawyer could try to make something of it. Collusion's the big thing today. How about talking with Ray? He interviewed them at the scene."

Wyatt and Renee had told Wilson that Sachs had practically choked their brother to death. However, they'd both been a little hazy about what caused the argument nor was there any mention of a chair having been thrown.

"I understand," Powers said. "Any word on Judd Pittway?"

Judd had been taken to a hospital in Baton Rouge, where he was expected to fully recover. He would be charged with one count of murder and three counts of attempted murder. An attorney had already been hired.

"He's in good hands," JT said. "Got a doctor and a lawyer. Soon's you finish looking through that briefcase," JT said to Powers, "I'll call Ray."

The briefcase had contained a copy of Dewitt Pittway's will. Ann Creely had run off another copy for Powers. Also of interest were a couple of credit card receipts from gas stations. One in Tallahassee and the other in Key Largo and both made on the day of Monica Kuun's homicide. Powers considered them a map to a murder.

"Anything you find at Sachs' place that has to do with your case," he continued, "I'll mark as part of the chain of evidence here and send it to you."

"That would be great, sir," Powers said.

She hadn't said anything to him about her phone call to Vicki.

"You ready to go, detective?" Wilson asked, knocking at the door.

~ ~ ~

The drive from Bonnet to Cleopus was short and fast. Wilson lit up the cruiser's roof rack to expedite the trip. Too bad Sachs hadn't had one on his car to clear traffic, Powers thought. Although he'd probably done just as well without it. The car JT had said Sachs owned turned out to be a Mercedes AMG, a wingless jet built for eating miles on the autobahn. Driving it from New Orleans to Key West would be as comfortable as flying first class.

Wilson pulled into the driveway. The house was a modest bungalow and looked well-kept. They went inside. Everything was pin-neat and placed just so. The furnishings were sparse but comfortable. A framed photograph of a middle-aged man and woman hung on the wall behind the sofa. A small roll-top desk stood against a wall to the side.

"That's a picture of Sachs' folks," Wilson pointed out. "His mom died not long after her husband."

Powers walked over to the desk and opened it. Pigeon-holed inside were several letters. Thumbing through them she discovered they were mostly bills. Power Company, house painter, a credit card statement – she ran down the list of charges on it. Her eye stopped at one entry. Ninety-three dollars from Magnetic Therapy Mattress Pads.

"Think it'd be all right if I took this?" she asked, handing the bill to Wilson.

"Shouldn't be a problem," he said, "but I'll have to check with the boss."

Powers rummaged through the desk drawers but found nothing else of interest. They went into the bedroom. A dresser there yielded only what one would expect but the closet held a shocking surprise. Standing in a corner was a shotgun.

"Jesus, that belonged to Mr. Sachs," Wilson said quietly. "I remember it was a Remington. We used to go bird shooting together. That's what he killed himself with."

"Why would anyone ever want to keep it?" Powers asked, horrified.

"People do strange things in times of grief," Wilson said, reaching in for the shotgun. "Think I'll take this thing back to the station for safekeeping until it's decided what's happening with the house. Someone could break in and steal it. Enough guns around without adding another."

"Good idea," Powers agreed. "I've seen enough here if you're ready to leave."

CHAPTER 37

JT WAS ON HIS WAY OUT of the office when Powers and Wilson returned. They filled him in on their visit to the house and Wilson put the shotgun in the evidence room, listing it as property. JT agreed to make a copy of Sachs' credit card statement and Powers told him she was leaving tomorrow. He invited her to dinner but she begged off, saying she had to write a report on Sachs and talk with her boss. She promised to stop by the station in the morning.

She drove back to the Belle Helen Inn, took a quick shower and ordered a pizza to be delivered to her room. While waiting for it to arrive, she went over her notes she jotted down while talking with Ray Wilson about his interview with Wyatt and Renee.

Powers had now read a copy of the will. She thought the scheme Sachs had devised was credible and diabolical. It certainly provided a motive for murder. And proved to her beyond doubt that Burton Sachs was insane.

The credit card statement listing the magnetic pad was damning evidence against both Burton Sachs and Monica Kuun. And the gas station receipts from the briefcase put Sachs in the Keys the day of Monica's homicide.

She thought about the elder Sachs' home – how his son had seemed to have made it into some kind of shrine – and had even kept the gun his father used in his suicide. It would be interesting to hear what a forensic psychologist would say about that.

She was happy to be wrapping up this part of the investigation. The experience hadn't been pleasant but then, homicide never is. Now there was just one more stop to make, in New Orleans.

The pizza arrived with a knock on the door.

~ ~ ~

Powers didn't get away as early as she'd hoped the next day. Chief Diana Brennen had come to the sheriff's station to thank her for saving both hers and the senator's lives. Then JT had bent her ear for another hour going over the investigation in the Sachs' homicide. She'd promised to give anything else he needed by affidavit. It was mid-afternoon before she arrived in New Orleans.

Navigating across the city, she soon came to the apartment building. She lucked out and found a vacant parking spot just beyond its entrance. The lobby was open but there was no doorman or anyone inside. A directory on the wall next to the elevator indicated the building was both commercial and residential. Burton Sachs was listed on the fifth floor, number 507. She pushed the up button.

The entire floor appeared to be residential. Sachs' apartment was at the end of the hall. She rang the doorbell. No one answered. She knocked softly. Still no response. Putting on a pair of latex gloves, she slipped the key she'd found at Pittway's into the lock and opened the door.

"Hello?" she called out.

Obviously no one was there and she stepped inside, quietly closing the door behind her.

The living room was large with a picture window at one end overlooking the city. The kitchen was off it, a breakfast bar separating the two areas. A hallway led to the bedrooms and baths.

Powers decided to start with the bedrooms.

She flicked on the lights in the first one. The bed was made and everything looked neat and orderly. She wondered if Monica had someone come in to clean or did the housework herself. She'd bet on a cleaning service. Might be something to look into.

She went to the closet. Inside were a couple of white terrycloth robes and matching slippers. Nothing more. The chest of drawers was completely empty, except for extra bedsheets and a blanket. This was apparently used as a guest room. She noticed the bedside table had a drawer and pulled it open. Inside were four packs of condoms.

The second bedroom was also in order but its closet was full of dresses. Powers took one off the rack. It looked to be Monica's size. It also looked expensive. She replaced it and ran her hand over the others and then shut the door. Why had Monica brought so few clothes with her to Pittway's? She looked through the dresser drawers. Bras, panties, some designer tee-shirts, three naughty little nighties. She rummaged around but came up with nothing.

The bedside table was identical to the one in the other room. She opened its drawer. A box of tissues. No condoms.

There were two bathrooms. Fresh towels folded on the racks in both. Empty medicine cabinets. A small storage closet in the hall contained a vacuum cleaner.

She went back to the kitchen.

The refrigerator was empty and there was nothing in the freezer. Assorted glassware and place settings filled the cabinets. Shoved under a work counter was a plastic trash can.

She pulled it out.

Lying at the bottom was a FedEx box with a mailing label from Magnetic Therapy Mattress Pads just like the one she'd received. Only this was addressed to Monica Kuun at this very apartment.

Absolutely stunning, Powers thought and remembered something else Gleason had told her...*nobody ever said crooks were smart*. She took a picture of the box in the trash can with her cellphone. And then another from farther back to include the kitchen. She would leave the box as is in the trashcan and carry it back to Key West.

Now a cold feeling of something sinister and ugly seemed to seep from the walls, depraved and wicked, ready to smear anyone who got too close.

She thought of Sachs in this room brooding about his father. How Pittway had driven the man to commit suicide. The unbearable grief of loss had then taken his mother. Madness overcoming him and revenge a viable solution. Planning one murder. Then another. How far does abandonment spread, she wondered?

Now the question was what should she do next? There was nothing here that would help the sheriffs' with their investigation. They'd eventually find out Sachs owned it as they pursued their inquiries. Should she let Wanda Kuun know this was where her daughter had lived? Would the woman even care?

She picked up the trashcan and walked out, pulling the door shut behind her.

CHAPTER 38

GLEASON STUCK HIS HEAD in Jay Halderman's office, a wolfish grin on his face.

"Think we can wrap up the Truman Annex double feature," he said. "Just got off the phone with Powers."

"She back on the island?"

Gleason went in and took a seat.

"On her way," he said. "Should get in tonight."

"So what's the story?"

Gleason shook his head.

"Unbelievable, Jay. You already know what happened to Burton Sachs."

"Powers should get a commendation for saving those peoples' lives."

"I agree. Anyway, before all that happened, she'd found a key and address book belonging to Monica Kuun. By the way, the sheriffs' department there really helped out. Maybe you could send them a letter or something thanking them."

"Good idea, Earl. Go on."

"Well, Powers followed up on the address book. Made some calls and eventually found out where Monica Kuun was living. Remember, her mother had said she'd moved. The key belonged to an apartment, which was owned by Sachs. She went there and guess what? Turns out the lady was not only an accessary to murder with Sachs but as we now know was also his victim."

"That's pretty dark."

"Powers also found a FedEx box in the apartment addressed to Monica Kuun from the mattress pad company. That's solid evidence. She bagged it and is bringing it back."

Halderman nodded with a smile.

"No problem with warrants, I'm guessing," he said.

"None needed." Gleason smiled. "Nothing to do with the New Orleans department. Same deal with the sheriffs."

Halderman smiled again.

"Buy you a cup of coffee, Detective?"

~ ~ ~

Jack's plane got into Miami early that afternoon. The flight from LA had been uneventful and he'd slept most of the way, having been up late the night before. His real estate company had closed a deal on some expensive commercial property and he'd taken everyone in the office to dinner.

Surprisingly, he hadn't seen Detective Laura Dalton. Neither had he called her the whole time he was in town. Not once. He had wished her well on her engagement – and meant it – when they'd spoken on the phone before he left Key West. He didn't want to intrude anymore. Simple as that.

The parking lot where the car carrier had dropped off his Jeep was a short taxi ride from the airport. He'd phoned that he'd be picking it up today.

"Your car's on row fifteen," the attendant said, handing Jack an envelope. "Here're the keys."

"I thought you'd have it out front, washed and all. Called that I was coming today."

"Nobody told me nothing."

The Jeep was a mess. Jack figured it must've ridden across the country on an open carrier. He remembered seeing a carwash on the way here. He could also top off the gas tank. Shouldn't hold him up for too long.

The engine started immediately, as if it were glad to see him.

~ ~ ~

Rachel Powers had driven almost to Gainesville before having to stop for the night. She'd been completely beat and no amount of energy drinks was going to give her another mile. She'd found a motel and crashed.

She'd awakened later than planned and, after a quick breakfast at a nearby fast-food, was soon on the Florida Turnpike heading to Miami. Traffic was light and by keeping an eye on the rearview mirror and her foot on the gas pedal, she should be in the Keys by late afternoon.

It'd be good to get home. She missed her routine. The familiar faces. Gleason, Halderman, even Jack Hunter. She smiled at the thought and shifted in her seat. Her back had been complaining. She guessed the massaging ride she'd taken in JT's Corvette was wearing off. But that was giving her an idea. Maybe she could consider a masseuse. Not a chiropractor. She'd been down that road. This time someone with educated fingers. One thing was for certain, she'd throw out the magnetic mattress pad!

Traffic began to slow as she approached Miami.

~ ~ ~

There'd been a line at the carwash but it'd been worth the wait. The Jeep looked like its old self. Jack had gone for the wax-wash special, which included dressing the tires. Gassed up and with the side curtains and top stashed in the back, he crawled with the rest of the traffic along US 1 through Coral Gables and on to Florida City.

At last he was in the Keys. And stopped in a line of traffic stretching farther than he could see. He sat drumming his fingers on the steering wheel. The car in front started to move, then hit the brakes. Move. Brake. Move. Then something about the car looked familiar.

Actually, the driver did. He recognized who it was and honked his horn.

~ ~ ~

Powers felt her bottom had gone to sleep. How much longer in this stupid car? And now some idiot behind her in a red Jeep was blowing his horn! As if she could do something about the traffic. Now he was flashing his lights!

She glared in the rearview mirror and was met by a lopsided grin.

MEET THE AUTHOR

Robert Coburn has worked at major advertising agencies in New York and Los Angeles. His ads have won top awards both nationally and internationally. He is an instrument rated commercial pilot and plays saxophone. He and his wife now live in Carmel, California.

ABSOLUTELY AMAZING eBOOKS

AbsolutelyAmazingEbooks.com
or AA-eBooks.com

www.ingramcontent.com/pod-product-compliance
Lightning Source LLC
Chambersburg PA
CBHW070503030726
47503CB00004B/1155